MEET ME IN
December

RACQUEL HENRY

RACQUEL HENRY BOOKS

Meet Me in December.

Copyright © 2023 by Racquel Henry. All rights reserved. No other part of this book may be reproduced in any form or by any electronic or mechanical means, including information storage and retrieval systems, without permission from Racquel Henry. This is a work of fiction. Names, characters, places, and incidents are the product of an author's imagination and are used fictitiously. Any resemblance to people, living or dead, businesses, events, or locales are strictly coincidental.

Published by Racquel Henry Books, a division of Henry Co.

First Edition.

Find more about Racquel and her books, please visit her website: www.racquelhenry.com.

ISBN (trade paperback): 978-1-959787-03-7
ISBN (ebook): 978-1-959787-02-0

Cover design by Natalie Henry-Charles at Pretty Peacock Paperie
Developmental Editing by Kristen Hamilton at Kristen's Red Pen
Proofreading by Jenn Lockwood Editing
Interior design by Book Obsessed Formatting

For The Unit always: Mommy, Daddy, Nat Nat, Jeffy, Ella, Roman, and Titan

Also for Giancarlo Fortuna, wherever you are.

OTHER TITLES BY RACQUEL HENRY:

Holiday on Park

Letter to Santa

Christmas in Cardwick

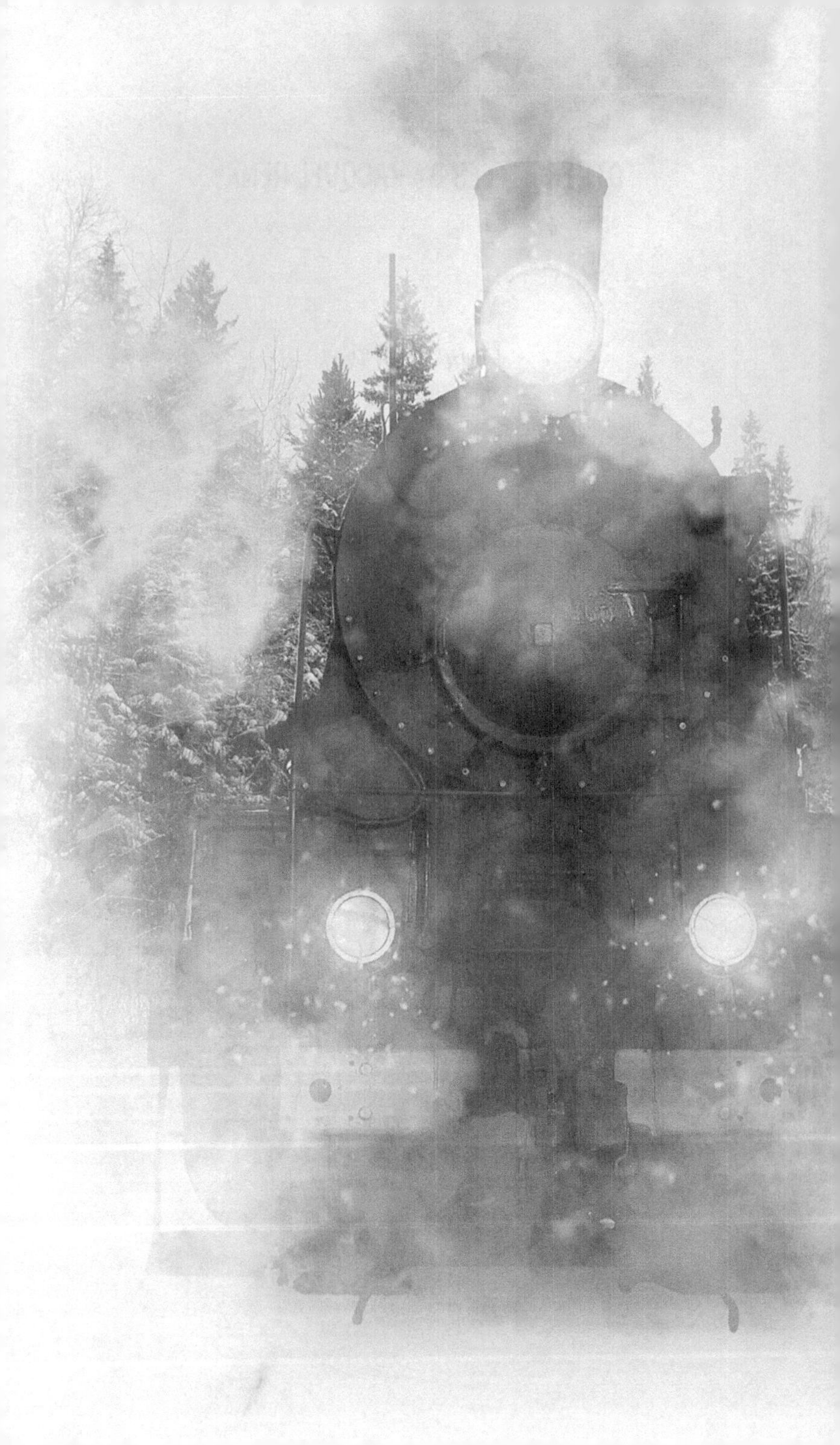

FELICITY

It's a good thing the human heart is not only durable, but elastic. Otherwise, I would have already dropped dead. This is the thought that orbited in my mind earlier as I walked through my old neighborhood. Taking the walk was supposed to clear my head after my boss shot down my ornament idea for the ninth time. And yes, I've counted. Instead, it was as if someone had taken a stack of old photos in the dust-covered trunk shoved to the back corner of my mind and dumped them at the front of it.

One remnant of my past is in every part of this town. He is splattered on building walls across Wedgefield, holiday banners, and in art prints sold at Miss Johnson's gift shop.

That remnant's name is Giancarlo Westbrook.

I'm still thinking about Giancarlo's murals around town and freezing my buns off after that walk while I hunt for one of Grams's special ornaments in her memory room. Grams's memory room—aka the name she gave her attic—isn't your average attic. There are no dusty cardboard boxes packed haphazardly with random junk items scattered across a dark room. There are no ghastly shadows that you're afraid things might be lurking in. It's more…comfy floral chair inviting you to sit with a cup of tea near a window overlooking a snow-covered garden. Instead of boxes, all her items are organized with labels in large, see-through, pink-tinted plastic containers. They sit on white utility shelves opposite the comfy chair. I stand in the warm glow from the overhead chandelier and think about how many Christmases my brother, Clay, and I came up here to look at old family photos.

I reach for the container labeled extra ornaments and lift the lid.

This Christmas will be a little different. Mom and Dad wanted to go home, so they're celebrating in Trinidad this year. Clay and I couldn't take off as much time from work as they wanted, so it was a no-go for us. Plus, Grams wasn't feeling up to making the trip.

As much as I'd love to be on our cozy island drinking ponche de crème and listening to parang music, I also don't want Grams to be alone.

I shuffle the ornaments in the bin, trying to find the exact glass-blown ornament Grams described, but nothing seems to match. I'm just about to reach for the lid to re-cover the container when a sliver of sparkly red tissue paper catches my eye. Maybe the ornament she wants is wrapped in that paper and she forgot.

I pick it up, and while I'm unwrapping it, a piece of creamy paper slips out and lands on my black winter boots. I bend down to retrieve it. Grams's handwriting is scrawled in black ink:

My Love,
Meet me on December 24th at our favorite bakery. I'll buy the croissants. Also, I made this for you. Hope you like it.
Xoxo,
Hazel

I flip the note over to see if there's anything on the other side, but it's blank. In the tissue paper, though, is a breathtaking ornament. It's intricate, very much like the handblown ornaments Grams taught me to make. It's got glittery swirls of silver and ice blue. Something she'd carefully crafted. There's a tiny tag on it that reads: *EB*

+ *HW*. I hook the ribbon of the ornament on my finger and hold it up in front of the window. In all my years of decorating the tree with Grams, I've never seen it. I put it back in the tissue paper, put the lid back on the bin, and head back downstairs.

Grams is taking a sip of hot chocolate from her favorite snowman mug while hanging a pinecone ornament on the tree. Her goal every year is to turn her house into a winter wonderland. It's already heavy on the stringed lights, fresh pine wreaths, and floral Christmas arrangements. The whole place smells like fresh cut Christmas trees, cinnamon, and clove. She sets down her mug and climbs up the step ladder. Her movements are a lot slower these days, but she's still as spunky as ever.

"Grams, I told you I would take the ones up top. The last thing we need right now is a slip and fall," I say.

"I'm old, Felicity, but I'm not dying." She glances at me and smirks. "At least not yet."

I shake my head. "That's not even remotely funny."

"Your brother is going to be here any minute now, and I'm way behind." She leans over the top of the step ladder, and I try not to have a heart attack.

"Grams, you do know there's no decorations deadline, right?" I move a little closer to the ladder to spot her, just in case.

"The sooner I get this all done," she says, reversing down the ladder, "the sooner I can kick my feet up and listen to the Mighty Sparrow's Christmas album."

I smile because that old Caribbean Christmas album was a staple throughout my childhood. My parents play it nonstop too.

Grams's foot comes down off the last step, and I breathe a sigh of relief when both feet are planted on the rug. But then her eyes land on the red sparkly tissue paper in my hand. I look down at it, forgetting I had it.

I clear my throat. "Oh, I was—"

She cuts me off. "What are you doing with that?" Her tone is condemning.

"I stumbled on this upstairs while looking for that ornament you wanted. I didn't mean to. It's just so pretty. I thought you might—"

"Put it back where you found it." She turns back to the tree so I can't see her face.

"Grams, I know I shouldn't be in your business…"

"Then why are you? Leave it alone, Felicity."

I fish out the note from the tissue paper and hold it up. "But this note seemed like it was important at one point."

She turns her head to the side, then glances over her shoulder. She breathes in deeply and releases the breath. "It was a long time ago."

"This is your handwriting. Who was he?"

She releases a deep breath, like it's been suspended in her lungs for decades, then takes a seat on the couch. Her deep brown eyes drift far away from here. "I once loved a boy."

"You mean other than Granddad?"

Her eyes dart to me, then away. "Yes. Contrary to what you and your brother think, I was young once. This was *before* your granddad. I went to study glass blowing in Italy. I wasn't planning on falling for anyone. It was supposed to be a fun college trip. I'd learn something new, and I'd be on my way. But he was there, and when I was with him, everything just...made sense."

I'm trying to process, because all I've ever known is this epic love story she and Granddad had, but now it sounds like what she's telling me is that it was more on the opening-act level. "Oh." It's all I can think to say while my brain does double Dutch. "Did you know him before your Italy trip?"

She smiles the kind of smile that makes the edges of her eyes expand. "Not personally. Wedgefield is a small town, so we all know of each other, but I never talked to him until that trip. Once I started, I couldn't stop. And I know what you're thinking. I loved your granddad, and I wouldn't trade my time with him for anything. My love for him gave me your father, which gave me you and Clay. But it's true. I almost went down a different road."

"I'm just trying to picture you falling for someone other than Granddad." I look down at the letter. "So what happened?"

"There's not much point in rehashing things. He's probably got his own life, just like I have mine. It wasn't meant to be."

"Grams, come on. It's me. I can tell by the way you're getting all worked up that he meant a lot to you. Haven't you ever wondered *what if?*"

She lets out a deep breath. "Of course I have." She gets that far-off look in her eyes again. "I was having trouble with some of the technique. He offered to stay late with me so I could practice. While all the other students were off having fun, he and I worked to perfect the craft. And then one night, we were in the studio late, and he kissed me." She chuckles. "That was my first kiss. My parents were stricter than yours. And if things had gone the way I wanted them to, I would have never kissed another man after that."

My grandfather was the love of her life, but the spark in her eyes and her words say something different. She might have loved Granddad, but there's a flame that's maybe been on low all this time. "So why didn't the two of you end up together?"

"Because of me," she says.

I raise an eyebrow.

"I never gave him that letter, as you can see. It just didn't feel like I fit into his life at that moment, and I thought it was best not to complicate things." She gets up and goes back to hanging ornaments on the tree. "I think that's enough. Please put it back where you found it."

"Grams—"

I want to get more answers, but the door bursts open then, and Clay is now traipsing into the living room, arms outstretched.

"Home for Christmas!" his deep voice booms through the living room.

I laugh, and Grams's face brightens again.

She crosses the space and cups his face in her hands, planting a kiss on his cheek. "Glad you made it, baby. You look as handsome as ever."

Clay envelops her in a giant hug. "Thanks, Grams. There's nowhere else I'd rather be."

"Well, it's good to see you're still alive," I say, stepping close enough for a hug.

"I know, sis. Sorry. It's been so hectic at work lately. We're launching a new line of sportswear at Star Athlete, and you know how it goes. We got a lot riding on it." He shrugs and flashes a warm smile—one that other people think mirrors my own.

Growing up, people would tell us we looked exactly the same, including our smiles. It never made sense to us. We're fraternal twins and neither of us think we look alike at all.

"I know. You could have at least responded with a quick text," I say.

"I'll try harder." He takes his coat off. "Listen, I had a last-minute change of plans."

Grams taps his shoulder. "Clayton James, you promised you'd be here for two weeks. If you—"

"No, nothing like that Grams. You'll like this change of plans. I brought a guest."

"Oh, you did?" I ask, craning my neck to see beyond him to the door. "Who is she?" But my heart stops instead when Giancarlo Westbrook, aka the remnant splattered on those familiar Wedgefield walls, sweeps in through the doorway, his carry-on in tow.

"Giancarlo!" Grams says, holding her arms open.

He pushes the handle of the carry-on down and leaves it at the door, then embraces Grams. "Been a while. But it's good to see you, Mrs. James."

"I almost can't believe it. Look at you. Even more of a cutie than the last time I saw you. Still have that twinkle in your eyes." She gives his scarf a tug.

She's not wrong about that twinkle. I memorized it well. The whole time I'm standing there, wondering why, out of nowhere, I don't even know how to blink anymore.

Giancarlo's eyes land on me, and it's not just my

eyes that don't work. Nothing else seems to work anymore. Not my eyes, not my brain, and certainly not my double-crosser heart. *We'll need to have a talk about that later, heart.*

"Hey, Felicity." He gives me a warm smile, and still nothing works.

It's only when Grams clears her throat that I snap out of it. "Hey, Giancarlo."

"It's good to see you," he says.

"Yeah. Same. I mean, it's nice to see you too." Since my brain won't form coherent sentences, I'll have to have a talk later with it too.

"Why don't you all get comfortable in the living room, and I'll grab some hot chocolate to warm us up? You can help me finish the decorating while we catch up," Grams says.

I've never been more grateful for an interception.

Everyone clears out, but Giancarlo glances over his shoulders, those sepia eyes I learned by heart lingering on mine. When they're all gone, I let out a long breath, and a flutter I didn't ask for runs through me.

In an early draft of us, Giancarlo is texting me that he's brought home my favorite pasta dish, which is lobster macaroni from The Golden Lobster. In this early draft, we eat said pasta while feeding each other secrets under the glittering Wedgefield sky. But as expected with all early drafts, we're rough around the edges. And when he leaves for art school, we become an unfinished draft, one we're both pretty certain is supposed to stay that way, tucked in a drawer never to see the light of day again. Sometimes, rough drafts are meant to stay rough drafts. Except for those stories that have a mind of their own. The stories that need time and space to sort themselves out. The stories that insist on being told.

GIANCARLO

If I had to rank a list of things I wasn't expecting, feeling a skip of the heart after laying eyes on Felicity James after six years would be number one million. Scratch that. It wasn't a skip. It was a jump of the heart—but also a guilt of the heart. We'd been good friends because of Clay, but after I left for art school, I didn't make much of an effort to keep the friendship going. There were separate reasons for that, and the kiss we shared on Christmas break six years ago didn't help things either. I'd learned early on that Felicity was a game I was never going to win. Still, I've wondered about what would have happened if I had. When my mind dips into wishing-I-had-put-in-the-effort territory, I force my thoughts to do an about-face until they're far enough away from her. That's the thing about your thoughts sometimes, though—they can be stubborn little antiheroes.

I drag both my hands down my cheeks. I wasn't going to be here that long. I'd handle being around her, just like I did for our whole childhood.

I look around the guest room that Mrs. James set up for me. It's decorated for Christmas, complete with red truck flannel sheets and a mini Christmas tree on the dresser. Pictures of the three of us—Clay, Felicity, and me—make up a collage of framed pictures on one of the walls. It's probably the only place in existence with pictures of me as a kid. I used to sleep in this same room when I spent the night. I was always looking for an excuse to escape my own home. Sometimes, Felicity and I would sneak out to look at the stars in the backyard. She would never tell me what she wished for when it was for herself, but I'd wish for my parents to get along. Often, she'd give up her wish to wish the same. When I asked her why she wasted her wishes on me, she'd say helping someone get their wish was never a waste. When I was with her, that part of my life didn't feel all that bad.

I shake the memory away because that's all it is. History. My phone buzzes in my pocket. I fish it out and groan when I see the name attached to the text message on the screen: Riley.

> **Riley:** *The blocked artist thing is real, but your unfinished mural is a bit of an eyesore. The mayor wants this done by the time we reopen the office for New Year's, and he's getting a little nervous.*

And then in another text:

> **Riley:** *Actually, we're all getting a little nervous.*

I let out a deep breath in a failed attempt to cleanse all the frustration from my body. It's the first time I've been blocked on a job. I've painted murals across the US—for famous people, even. But for some reason, I just couldn't figure out the story I wanted my art to tell for this particular project. I jumped at Clay's offer to come to Wedgefield for a few days to clear my head, and I'd explained to Riley that I was blocked and needed some space. I stupidly thought that was going to be good enough. I type out a quick message back to Riley:

> **Giancarlo:** *The mayor will have his mural.*

At least, I sure hope so.

Maybe I need more hot chocolate. I could grab a cup since everyone had gone their separate ways after we finished helping Mrs. James decorate. I should be able to slip in and out of the kitchen. Then I can sit down to sketch. There has to be something worthy in this brain of mine. I put on my green plaid pajama pants and slip a white t-shirt over my head before heading downstairs.

When I round the corner to the kitchen, I'm wrong about Operation Hot Chocolate being an easy mission, because Felicity is standing with her back leaning against the counter, pink reindeer mug in hand, and reading something on her phone. My eyes drift to her bare legs, which are crossed. Her bronze skin shimmers under the overhead light.

Why couldn't this just be an easy trip? I take a few steps toward her, and she gasps when she sees me, placing a hand on her chest.

"Didn't mean to scare you," I say.

"Oh, no. I was just lost in the world of glass-blown ornaments," she says.

"Looks like we had the same idea." I nod to her mug.

She clicks her phone off and straightens. "Reminds me of…"

"Late-night hot chocolate chats on Christmas break?" I finish. It was one of the many things we did as kids, mostly around the holidays, and Clay was usually with us.

We both laugh. I've missed that laugh. It was like a favorite Christmas song. It could make anyone happy, and you wanted to play it on repeat.

"How's that going?" I ask.

She wrinkles her eyebrows in the same cute way she always used to, and suddenly I'm seventeen again.

"The glass blowing. Clay said you work at Muralo in Ivanhoe Springs now?"

"Yeah." She takes a sip of her hot chocolate.

I study her and can't help but notice her eyes don't get the same glow they did all those years ago when she'd talk about being an ornament maker for Muralo. "Isn't that what you always wanted?"

She half smiles. "It is. But it's just that, lately, something feels off. I've been there for five years, and I still can't get my boss to take me seriously."

I reach up and open the cabinet where Mrs. James keeps the mugs. "What do you mean? I can't imagine anyone *not* taking you seriously," I say. Because I can't. I've always taken her seriously, which was the least I could do since I couldn't have her.

Another half-smile. "Thanks, Giancarlo."

I look back at her from where I am at the cabinets and smile. She's the only person on this planet who calls me by my full name—well, aside from my father when he's angry with me. When we were teenagers, I asked Felicity one night why she didn't use my nickname like everyone else. She gave me two reasons. First, she liked my whole name. Second, she always liked not being like everyone else. I wasn't sure if she meant in general or not being like everyone else *to me*, so I just nodded and took another bite of pasta.

The memory fades when she breaks my thoughts with, "I have all these ideas, but she doesn't want to change anything. She wants us to keep doing the same things because 'why *mess with a good thing?*' Her words, not mine. She just shot down another idea, so I sent her another. Now I'm waiting for her next Negative Nancy email." She twirls a finger around her curly brown hair. She still has all the same habits, and part of me wishes she didn't, because everything reminds me of that unspoken territory we lived in when we were younger. I'd already traveled out of there, and I'm not supposed to be taking any trips back.

"So do your own thing." I pour the hot chocolate from the thermos into my mug.

She rubs her cheek. "I can't just do my own thing. Do you know how expensive the equipment is for glass-blown art? I mean, the kiln alone..." She shakes her head.

I drop a few marshmallows in my cup and stir, but then stop, the spoon clinking against the mug. I move so I'm standing in front of Felicity. She's staring down into her mug. She's barely looked at me since I got in, and now the thought that she might be mad at me for how I let things slip zips through my mind.

I put my index finger under her chin, and in the

softest way, push her chin up so her eyes have to meet mine. It's the closest I've been to her in six years, and even though my brain wishes it's enough time to forget what that's like, my heart insists on operating on muscle memory. When she's around, it *knows*.

"You've always been the smartest person I know. If there's anyone who can find a way, it's you." I don't move my hand.

"I am?" she says, her voice only a decibel above a whisper.

"Yeah, you are." This time, I back off before I can't stop myself from losing control.

"Midnight hot chocolate. Just like old times." Clay's voice fills the room, overpowering any trace of emotion that was in the room a second ago—and it's probably for the best.

Felicity hurries over to the sink, which is as far away from me as she can get in the room. "Except, it's not midnight," she says as she turns on the faucet.

Clay laughs. "Yeah, well, we're a lot older now. These days, nine-thirty feels like midnight." He glances at both of us, then grabs his own mug. "Can't believe you two were trying to have midnight hot chocolate without me."

Felicity laughs, and there's nothing I can do about stopping the high and low of it from taking a shot at my heart. I'd done my best to forget that sound.

"Jealous much?" Felicity says.

"Nah," Clays says, picking up the thermos of hot chocolate. "Just a case of FOMO."

"Missing out on what?" Felicity asks, amused.

Clay shrugs. "You two were always closer"—he looks at me—"even though Gi is *my* best friend."

Felicity's gaze flicks to me, both of us looking away at the same time.

Clay takes a sip of his hot chocolate. "I was always stuck at basketball practice or games. So unfair how much y'all got to hang out without me. And we all know I'm the best part of this friend group."

We all laugh. It's all I can do because my brain is still stuck on his comment about Felicity and me being closer. I didn't think he noticed. And I thought I had worked hard to keep that information confidential. Felicity and I never talked about our hangouts together. Neither one of us needed to say we shouldn't broadcast it. We just kind of knew.

Felicity makes her way over to Clay and smacks his arm. "Thought you'd be over yourself by now," she says.

"Never, sis," Clay says.

She shakes her head, curls bouncing everywhere. "As much as I'd like to stay here and listen to The Clay Show, I'm going to turn in."

Clay smirks. "Well, you'll miss tonight's episode, but

you can always tune in again tomorrow."

Felicity shakes her head before her eyes land on me. "Night, Giancarlo. Really good to have you home."

"Thanks. Good to be home," I say, forcing myself to peel my eyes away because I almost forgot Clay is in the room. But that's how it always is when she's around. Everything holding me together inside scatters, and mostly, I can't see anyone else. All the distance and time apart was my way of intentionally throwing water on the fire. It was supposed to snuff all that out. The lie detector test determined that was a lie.

Once she leaves the room, I avert my eyes to my mug so Clay can't see how out of sorts I am. As much as I'd like to deny it, it's not just Wedgefield or Clay's grandmother's house that feels like home.

FELICITY

Of course Clay would invite Giancarlo to come back home with him and not disclose that vital information to anyone—specifically, to me. Grams always said *the more the merrier*, but still. It's common courtesy. And now I've lost sleep over it too. I yawn and stretch my arms to the ceiling. Since Grams got all huffy the yesterday about her secret lover, and I needed a distraction from the incredibly gorgeous half-Italian man staying in the next room over, I made up my mind last night that my mission, which I'd chosen to accept, would be to find this mystery lover. Do I have any idea how I am going to do that? Nope. But I have to try. I can't let go of the fact that maybe, just maybe, Grams had missed out on the love of her life. Of course I don't want to take away from Granddad, but the idea of "wrong timing" fascinates me—not that I'm speaking from personal experience.

I glance at the time: 7 AM. Probably just Grams would be up, but I could easily grab a cup of coffee and escape her if I told her I had work stuff to do. I ease my door open and listen for any noise. Silence. As I tiptoe down the hall, trying to be quiet, the door to the hallway bathroom creaks open, and out steps Giancarlo.

My brain tells me to abort mission, but I can't move because what's in front of me now is endless skin. Everywhere. Or at least, that's all my eyes focus on. His muscles are still glistening from the water droplets he's clearly missed, a white towel slung over his shoulder. A loose wave of his dark-brown hair hangs in his sepia eyes. For a moment, the two of us stare back at each other, wide-eyed. Well, I'm the one with the wide eyes.

Giancarlo smiles and says, "Morning."

I blink. Physically, I'm standing in front of him. Mentally, I'm on a word hunt.

"Felicity?"

It's my own name that snaps me out of it. I swallow. "Hmm?"

He smiles again. "I said, morning."

Right. "Morning, Giancarlo!" It comes with a bit too much pep, but I'm not about to give him the chance to notice, because I'm already speed-walking to the steps. I reach up and touch my hair, then curse myself when I remember I'm a mess. I shouldn't even be this pressed. It's just Giancarlo. So what if I had a thing for him? That was years ago. YEARS. Besides, it wasn't possible then, and it isn't possible now.

"Why do you look like The Ghost of Christmas Past came to visit you last night?" Grams says when I reach the kitchen. She's sitting in her breakfast nook and the sparkly garland framing the window gleams behind her.

I gasp and jump slightly.

"Felicity, what on earth has gotten into you?"

I let out a deep breath and place my hand on my chest to steady myself. "Nothing, nothing. You just scared me."

"I do live here, you know. And there are two other humans in this house, counting the Christmas ghost of past." She winks and brushes a gray curl out of her eye.

I stare at her with my mouth hanging open for a few beats, then say, "What is that supposed to mean?" Even though I'm pretty sure I know what she's getting at. She always had a sharp eye, which to this day I prefer to ignore.

"Not a thing," she says, sipping her morning coffee.

I roll my eyes and pick up the coffee pot. "Listen,

Grams, about the other day... The ornament—"

"Felicity, don't go there." She picks up her tablet, which has her latest romance novel pulled up on the screen. She does a lot of reading in general, but reading over coffee is one of her favorite morning rituals.

"But, Grams."

"I mean it, Felicity. I haven't even finished my first cup of coffee, and already you're playing Nancy Drew—Love Detective Edition."

I wrinkle my brows. "That's not a thing."

"It is now." She puts on her readers, then looks at me over the top of them. "I don't want you opening chapters in books that are already closed. Okay?"

I purse my lips, then give the slightest nod. I should respect her wishes, and I usually want to, but if I have an unsettling feeling about it, then she must. The both of us can't miss out on the one we want.

Later that day, when Grams goes to her best friend, Ms. Nettie's, birthday party, I flop down on her velvet couch in the living room and open my laptop. The warm white lights from the tree catch my eye, and I let my gaze linger on it before diving into my research. There are only two bakeries in Wedgefield: Snapdragon Bakery and

Crystal's. Grams always refused to go to Snapdragon, so that math isn't hard there. I open my laptop and type in the name. I honestly don't know what I'm looking for or who I think I am. I'm definitely no Nancy Drew. Still, my heart tells me that this was and still is important to Grams. She'll thank me later.

Just as I'm scrolling through the menu and salivating over croissants, the hairs on the back of my neck stand at attention. Giancarlo's face appears over my shoulder. My heart does its standard double-time march, the one I try to get down to adagio every time Giancarlo is around.

"Hungry?" he asks, his face still inches from mine. He's looking at the screen, but when I shift just a little to look at him, his eyes lock with mine. He. Is. *Close.* I try not to go back to teenage versions of us—the versions that were magnetic. The very ones who fought with every fiber to stay apart.

When Giancarlo tucks one of my loose curls behind my ear, I swallow. His eyes are like a city you want to get lost in during autumn. They are kaleidoscope shades of brown with a side of moodiness. I turn my head back to the computer screen.

"When it comes to croissants, I'm not messing around."

He flashes a smile. Meanwhile, I am internally begging my heart to slow its tempo.

"You planning on heading there?" He nods to the

laptop.

"No, I, um…" My brain is blank. I don't know that Grams would appreciate me sharing this secret.

Giancarlo narrows his eyes. "I know that look on your face."

"What look?" I try to relax the muscles in my face.

"That one." He points his index finger at me. "It's been a few years, but I still know you pretty well. You've never been any good at lying."

I wrinkle my brows.

"Not to me, anyway." We hold each other's gaze for a few beats before he breaks it and sits on one of the velvet armchairs across from me. I let out a deep breath. Him being in the same town, in the same house this Christmas, is already hard enough. If he keeps getting close to me, I might not make it out of here alive. So much for hearts being durable.

"I'm working on Christmas gifts," I say. It's not a total lie. I want to find Grams's Mystery Lover before Christmas, and no matter what she says, I know it's the ultimate gift. Plus, you don't just keep special things without reason. That ornament, wrapped so carefully in pretty tissue paper, is her sliver of hope that she might see Mystery Lover again someday.

Giancarlo rests his arms on his thighs and leans forward. And now I have the best view of his toned arms under the form-fitting sweater he's wearing.

It would be nice if he could help me out and stop being so...attractive. I need to be out of his orbit. It's like being teenagers all over again. I don't even know how I made it through all those years growing up.

"Felicity?" he says.

I blink, my thoughts evaporating when I register that I've been staring. "Um, sorry. What did you say?"

He laughs. "I said, what did you get me?"

I try not to smile, but the corners of my lips refuse to cooperate. "Who says I'm getting you anything? I didn't even know you were coming."

He nods and looks at the floor then back to me. "Is it okay that I'm here?"

A wave of something I'm not sure of spirals through me. "Why wouldn't it be okay?"

He shrugs. "I was already debating if I should come. I don't want to be in anyone's way." His eyes drill into mine.

I swallow. My brain screams at me to look away, look anywhere but those city eyes. But I can't. Part of me is frustrated with time. Time is supposed to be the miracle wound healer and from the second Giancarlo entered this house, it's been clear that *nothing, nothing, nothing* has healed for me.

"You'd never be in anyone's way in this house," I say. Our eyes are still locked on each other, my body an entire planet of longing.

"She's right, Gi," Clay says, entering the living room. "You know this is the one place you never have to worry about that stuff, man."

I drop my gaze to the computer screen, and Giancarlo leans back in his chair, shifting his attention to Clay.

"Thanks," Giancarlo says. "You know, your grandmother's house felt more like home than my actual home."

Clay claps Giancarlo on the back before taking a seat on the armchair next to him. "And I wouldn't have it any other way. You're family."

I give a quick glance up from my screen and smile. Clay has always been protective of his friendship with Giancarlo. It's another reminder that all we can ever be is friends. Although we've never said it out loud, it's the reason we've both actively worked to keep that early draft of us locked in a drawer. *The kiss* had changed everything and nothing at the same time.

Clay studies me for a beat before asking, "So, what you workin' on?"

"Christmas gifts, apparently," Giancarlo says. His eyes twinkle with mischief.

"Okay, I'm not going to go through this whole trip with the two of you ganging up on me," I say.

They both laugh.

"Have you thought about a gift for Grams yet?" Clay asks.

I press my lips together. Really, I'm trying to think of a lie. Meanwhile, all eyes in the room are on me. Not helping.

Clay tilts his head to the side. "You've been acting a little strange since we got here. What gives?"

Giancarlo looks away, and I shrug, mainly hoping it will buy me time to come up with something.

"Felicity." Clay has always been able to call me out.

I glance around. "Is Grams still out at Ms. Nettie's birthday party?"

Clay nods, his face scrunching up from all my secrecy.

"Okay, I wasn't going to bring this up, but I found something in the attic yesterday."

Clay wrinkles his brows and folds his arms. "Not exactly breaking news, sis. There are lots of old family relics in the attic to discover."

I roll my eyes. "I know that, genius. Let me finish." I tell him the story about what I found and how Grams got all twitchy about it.

After I get done, Clay leans back in his chair. Giancarlo runs a hand through his dark waves.

"There was another dude before Granddad?"

Again, I roll my eyes. "Women can date multiple men in their lifetimes, you know. Kind of like your revolving door of women."

Giancarlo's eyes go wide, and a smirk plays at his lips.

Clay lets out a deep breath. "I just haven't found the one. At least I've got *something* going on in that department."

I push my shoulders back. "And how do you know I don't?"

Giancarlo drops his smile then, his eyes boring into me again.

"Whatever," Clay says. "I didn't mean it like that, anyway. I just meant it's hard to believe because I thought Granddad was her person."

I nod. No argument there.

"So what's your plan?"

"I know this sounds wild, but my gut tells me this is important. Like it's something she's only kept a lid on because of fear." I click the little star on my browser to bookmark the bakery webpage.

Clay is quiet for a few seconds before saying, "Okay, I'm in."

"Whoa. I already told you she doesn't want me solving this mystery, so you need to act like you never heard what I just told you," I say.

"And I will, but I can help. And Gi can too."

"Wait, what?" Giancarlo and I say at the same time.

Clay sits up straighter. "I can distract Grams and keep her busy while you and Gi figure this out. Admit it, she's already pretty sharp. She'll notice what you're up to if she has nothing to do."

Of course he's right, but still. "Yeah, but why does Giancarlo have to—"

"Yeah," Giancarlo says at the same time. "I'm just here to clear my head."

Clay holds up both of his hands. "If you're trying to find Mystery Lover by Christmas, then it might be faster if you both work on it. And I'll help where I can."

"Or maybe you're just trying to impose on my present to Grams so you don't have to think of something to get her," I challenge.

Clay smiles. "Well, that *would* be an added perk."

I shake my head.

"Aside from the obvious spirit of gift giving, I think you're right that this might be important to Grams." Clay turns to Giancarlo. "So, you in, Gi?"

Giancarlo juts his chin at me. "You good with this, Felicity?"

No, I want to say. I'm not good with this. The draft is supposed to stay in the locked drawer. It's a story that isn't supposed to be told.

"Uh, yeah," I say, meeting his eyes.

"Excellent," Clay says, relaxing his back against the chair again.

Suddenly, I'm not so sure about the reliability of that lock.

GIANCARLO

Come with me to Wedgefield, Clay said. *You need a change of scenery*, Clay said. *You'll be able to clear your mind*, Clay said. Since I walked through that front door and saw Felicity James, my mind has been nothing but a briar patch of memories. They are memories I like, but one false move and I might get stuck. Or worse, both of us will get hurt. I'm already having a hard enough time concentrating on anything other than the fact that she challenged Clay yesterday about her dating life. Of course I didn't expect her to stay single. A million guys must want her, but it didn't change that I never stopped wanting her. Even if I can't have her, I don't want to know that she's inspiring another man's heart.

I'm about to put my phone in my jacket pocket when it buzzes in my hand. Riley's name appears across the screen, and the usual sink in my stomach follows. I tap the screen to open up the text.

Riley: *Any progress on those ideas?*

I groan, then think for a second.

Giancarlo: *I'm off to regroup, Riley. Just a reminder that your office cleared it.*

She's acting like I just took off and abandoned my job. If I'd have known she was going to text me every two seconds, I would have just stayed put.

Riley: *I know. But Mayor Ortiz asked me to keep checking in.*

It's not like I hadn't turned in sketches at their requested deadline. It just so happened the mayor said none of my ideas were "it."

Riley: *I'm just making sure you're staying on top of it. We don't have a lot of time. The mayor wants this done by the time the office reopens after New Year's.*

Giancarlo: *Do you trust me?*

The text bubbles move back and forth, then drop,

then move back and forth. The cycle repeats a few times.

> **Riley:** *We trust you.*

> **Giancarlo:** *The mayor will have his mural.*

I switch the off button. Her hesitation isn't very reassuring.

I head downstairs to the entryway and pull on my coat. Just as I place my scarf around my neck, Felicity comes down the steps. I have to remind myself not to stare, but it's hard. She's the kind of woman who never enters a room quietly, even though she hasn't said a thing. Her spirit is so vibrant you *have* to look. There's no such thing as looking away.

She smiles. "Ready?"

"Yeah," I say. I pause, then say, "You look nice." I probably shouldn't say it, but friends can tell each other they look nice.

"Thanks." She reaches for her red peacoat, but I beat her to it and hold it out for her to put on. She pauses but allows me to help her. She slides an arm in one of the sleeves, and then the other. I fix the coat so it's up on her shoulders, and when she turns back to face me, she says, "Always the gentleman." Her eyes linger on mine for just a beat longer than they should, but she looks away before it turns into a moment. "Grams, we're running to the store. Be right back," she calls before opening the front door.

And then we're out in the cold, walking to the sidewalk to wait for our rideshare. I take in all the cottage-style homes lining the street, and nostalgia washes over me. Most of the neighborhood decorates for Christmas, so there are various lawn displays in each yard. I check across the street for the Garcia family's Santa sleigh with glowing reindeer, and smile. It was always my favorite growing up, and after all these years, it makes me happy that the tradition continues.

At first, Felicity and I are quiet. I try to think of what to say. I want to tell her everything, just like when we were kids. I know everything about her, and yet, now I know nothing.

Instead of asking her to tell me everything, like I want to, I talk about the ride instead. "The app said the car should be here in under a minute."

"I hope so because I'm freezing," she says.

I nod. Now that I've said the one thing I can think of, I'm back to square one. Will the whole trip be like this?

Felicity clears her throat. "How's the muralist life going?"

I groan.

"That bad, huh?"

"No, no. It's just…I came here to try and clear my

head. I've got this big project in Marvelwest for the mayor, and his office has been on my case to finish, but I've been creatively blocked."

"That doesn't sound like you."

"I know. It's the first time I've been on an assignment and not been able to perform."

"The answer is often right in front of you," she says.

"If only I could see it," I say.

"You will." She waits a few beats before asking, "So how're your folks?"

It's not always my favorite topic, because things are complicated with my parents—always have been. Felicity helped me live through it growing up. "Still don't hear from my mom much. I've given up on expecting something different from her. Dad is good."

"Heard he moved to Florida a few years ago. He still there?" Felicity asks.

"Yup." I run a hand through my hair. "It suits him. He never liked the cold, but he moved to Wedgefield for Mom."

Felicity touches my arm, giving it a slight shock. "I'm sorry about your mom."

I shrug. "It's okay. After one too many disappointments, you live with it."

"But you shouldn't have to."

Her eyes are on mine for a split second, but our ride

arrives. I open the back door to the sleek, black sedan, and Felicity slides in. I do the same. Though we're now in the car, mentally I'm in the middle of that split second when it feels like that look in her eyes is only for me, the place I wish I could stay a little longer.

It's not a far drive, but we decided that it was too early for walking in the cold. We're quiet most of the way, the gentle hum of the engine filling the gaps between our silence and my mental pictures of Felicity in the arms of other men. I have no business asking her about it, though.

"There you are," she says, splitting the quiet as we pass the Wedgefield Museum.

It's one of my earlier space-inspired murals. I sometimes still can't believe my art is just out there in the world for people to look at. A young Giancarlo had no idea this was even possible.

"You're everywhere," Felicity says.

Something about the way she says it makes me think that it bothers her. I want to ask, but the car stops, and we arrive in front of Snapdragon Bakery. Once I hop out, Felicity slides over, and I hold my hand out to help her. She stares at it for a few seconds, and I think she's going to tell me that she doesn't need any help, but at last she takes it. For a brief moment, I pretend she's mine and imagine how I'd hang on while we walk to the door. But that fantasy dissipates because she drops my hand almost right away. I'm fine.

Inside, it's quiet, and there's only one other customer when we walk through the glass door. The place doesn't look all that different since I was in here last. The walls are painted white now instead of the buttery yellow that I remember, but the same old photos line the walls, and they still have the same dark-wood furniture. Felicity studies the display case while we wait for the one customer to finish with their order.

"How about a croissant?" I ask her.

She looks up at me like she's in a bit of a fog.

I can feel that she's about to tell me no, so I intercept her thought with, "Come on, we have to buy something anyway. We can't just walk in here and start asking the man questions without at least buying something."

She smiles, which makes my heart miss a beat, but I shake it off. I have to remember there's no end game here. Still, I can't take my eyes off her. There's always been a part of me that wanted to memorize everything about her, and right now, I'm fighting hard to keep that part of me locked away where it's supposed to be.

The guy behind the counter bends down to retrieve a stack of boxes from under the counter, his dark, gelled hair peeking out right at the counter height. He sets the boxes down behind him on top of another counter and waves to us. His nametag says *Carmine*.

"How may I help you?" Carmine says.

"Hi, Carmine," Felicity says. "We're hoping to take a box of your croissants to go. They look amazing."

Carmine reaches for a red-and-green-striped pastry box. "Thank you. We bake them fresh every day."

Felicity gives me a quick glance, and I nod to urge her to keep going.

"I was also wondering if you could help us with something else as well." She tucks one of her loose curls behind her ear.

Carmine is placing croissants in the box, but he stops and looks up at Felicity. "What's that?" His thick eyebrows knit together.

"I was wondering if you knew anything about the family that used to own the bakery," Felicity says.

Carmine narrows his eyes. "Why?"

I laugh and hold two hands up. "Don't worry, we grew up in Wedgefield. We're actually trying to track down someone her grandmother lost touch with." I point at Felicity.

"Ah, I see." He finishes piling croissants into the box, then sets it on the counter. "To be honest, I don't know a lot about them. My family bought the bakery when I was pretty young."

"So you don't know anyone with the initials EB that might have owned the bakery?" I ask.

He shakes his head. "It was a long time ago. I could ask my parents to see if they have any memory or paperwork?"

"Oh, could you? That would be great," Felicity says, reaching into her purse. "Here's my card. You can email me or call me if you find out anything," she says.

"Of course." Carmine goes back to packaging the croissants and ringing them up. I look over at Felicity, and her eyes are roaming over the old photos on the wall. She is stunning even when she does the simplest things.

I reach for my wallet in my back pocket. "I got this if you want to go take a closer look."

She nods and strolls over to a wall on the other side of the restaurant. Just as I'm writing in the tip for Carmine, the sound of something crashing to the floor with a thud fills the air. My head snaps in Felicity's direction.

"Are you okay, ma'am?" Carmine asks, leaning over the counter and craning his neck in her direction.

She's bending over and picking up one of the photo frames. When she stands up, she's clutching it tight, her eyes wide. "I—I'm sorry. It slipped out of my hands."

"What is it?" I ask.

"This… It's Grams," she says, her voice a hair above a whisper.

I hurry up and sign my name on the slip of paper, then make my way over to where she is. Standing next to her, I'm close enough to catch a hint of that rosy perfume she loves, and I try to focus as she hands me the dark-gold frame.

It is without a doubt Grams. She looks to be in her early twenties, and she's sitting in one of the booths with a man around the same age. He's got one arm slung over her shoulders. "They look—"

"Cozy?" Felicity finishes.

"I was going to say happy, but cozy works too," I say.

She grabs the frame from my hands and marches up to the counter. "Do you know the guy in this photo?" Felicity asks Carmine.

Carmine wrinkles his brows and takes the frame that Felicity practically shoves into his hands. What I've always liked about her is that when she's determined, nothing can stop her. And I love the way her face gets all serious when she wants something.

"Sorry, I really wish I could help, but I have no idea who these people are."

Felicity's shoulders shrink. "The woman in the photo is my grandmother." She uses her whole hand to gesture to the frame, then drops it so it rests on the counter.

"And we're thinking the guy in the photo probably has the initials E.B.," I say, heading over to them. I stand close to Felicity again, hoping to catch another trace of rosy perfume. I do, and I have to take a step back to get a hold of myself.

"He doesn't look familiar at all. But like I said, my parents might have more info," Carmine says.

Felicity pulls her phone out of her pocket and hits the camera button. "Would you mind if I take a picture of it with my phone?"

"No problem." Carmine hands the frame back to Felicity, and his eyes flick to the wall.

Taking the hint, Felicity quickly captures her own photo and places the frame back where she found it.

"Thank you for answering our questions." I pick up the pastry box on the counter and hold it up. "And for the croissants."

Carmine nods, then busies himself with wiping down the counters.

Felicity meets me at the front doors, and we both head out.

"Should we walk for a bit, get some fresh air?" Really, I'm nowhere near ready to go back to the house, and even though it's cold, I just want to keep hanging out with her.

"That has to be our mystery man," she says, moving down the sidewalk and not answering my question.

"So what now, Nancy Drew?"

"Nancy would know what to do next. I have no idea." The corners of her mouth turn down, and I try to focus on all the lampposts wrapped in garland ahead of us instead. I don't want to get wrapped up in the study of her lips. I've already taken that test, and it went a little too well.

"What I know about you is that when you want to get something done, you'll find a way," I say.

She smiles, but it disappears right away. "Not these days."

Her eyes land on the box of croissants in my hand, and she stops to open it and take one out. I do the same.

I take a small bite, then say, "Care to elaborate?"

She shrugs. "I've tried so many times to show my boss I'm ready to do something new with the ornaments we produce and take on more responsibilities at the company." She pauses and sighs. "Let's just say they won't be giving me the corner office anytime soon."

The wind is frigid against my cheeks. "Do you accept that?"

"What choice do I have?"

"It's like I was telling you in the kitchen. Maybe this is the universe's way of telling you to take a chance."

"I've thought about it. But it's expensive to get a business up and running. Plus, I'd have to give up a lot."

"Like what?"

"Healthcare, security—you know, basics." She purses her lips.

"If there's anything I've learned, it's that nothing is truly ever guaranteed, so you might as well jump."

She stops and faces me. "I wish it were that easy."

I stop too, and now our eyes are locked—not a key in the world can unlock them.

"It could be," I say.

"Sometimes outside forces are too strong, and it doesn't matter how bad you want something." She doesn't take her eyes off me.

"I'm a firm believer that if you want it bad enough, not a single outside force can stop it." It's then I notice my heart hammering in my chest.

For a few moments, it's just us standing in the cold, in the middle of the sidewalk. But something snags in Felicity's mind, and she blinks. And just like that, the two of us are back in Wedgefield and away from wherever we were a moment ago.

I smile. "We might not know what to do next about Mystery Lover, but there is one thing we need to do before we go back to your grandmother's house."

She tilts her head to the side. "What?"

"Eat these croissants before your grandmother catches us with this box."

"Now that I can do."

We both laugh, and it makes me realize that I haven't done a lot of that in a while. My home life wasn't always that great, but Felicity always made me laugh. She'd remind me that, even in all the chaos, there was still room to be happy. Maybe that reminder is why I needed to come home.

FELICITY

My heart is still recovering from the conversation with Giancarlo yesterday on the sidewalk. It's like we disappeared into some alternate timeline—one only we know. And normally, I wouldn't assume things, but I got the feeling we weren't only talking about my career wants. Being around him again is going to wreck me. It would be so much easier if I hated him. If he was the almost-ex that broke my heart. But he's not. He's the boy who brought me my favorite pasta and watched stars with me for hours. It's not his fault that I fell for him. And it's still not his fault that there's a part of me still clinging to that first draft of us. I wish he made it easier for me to *not* want him.

My phone dings, and I'm thankful for something—anything—to save me from confronting my truth. I smile when I see my friend Juliet's name appear on the screen. Juliet and I met a few years back while she was on a work trip. She was one of those fancy LA types but ended up moving back to her hometown of Orlando to be closer to her high school sweetheart, Ivan.

Juliet: *Omg, girl. I love the ornament you made to commemorate my anniversary with Ivan! I can't wait for him to see it!*

Felicity: *Yay! Was nervous you wouldn't like it.*

Juliet: *I wouldn't have asked you to do it if I didn't already love your work!*

Felicity: *Aww, thanks, love.*

Juliet: *Of course. I still think you need to do this yourself. Your ornaments are too special. My mom loved the one you made for her last year too.*

Felicity: *That makes me so happy.*

Juliet: 🖤 *Do it! Thanks again!*

Felicity: 🖤

It's not that I doubt my work, but it's not a sure thing. There are so many things to get in place before that kind of leap. I prefer to see what's in front of me before I jump.

There's a soft knock on the door, and I am once again grateful for any distraction that will stop my brain from spinning circles.

"Come in," I say. I'm lying on the floor, still staring up at the ceiling, when I feel him enter. I always sense his heart first.

"Everything okay?" he asks.

Guess my brain will keep spinning circles for all eternity—or at least while the two of us are still in this town. I turn my head to see Giancarlo standing in the doorway, a brown bag with a lobster outline in his hands. I immediately sit up and point to the bag. "Is that—"

"Lobster macaroni?" He grins.

I gasp. "You didn't."

"I did." He takes a seat on the floor next to me.

I try not to notice the way being near him makes the hairs stand straight up across my whole body, or the way that internal nervousness takes the form of shooting stars.

"I figured it was too cold to sit outside like we used to in the summer."

I nod because I'm still trying to find the words. It's like being sixteen, and I'm not prepared for the way that makes me feel.

Giancarlo tilts his head to the side. "If you're busy…"

"I'm not busy," I blurt out. "It's just…it reminds me of a time."

"Yeah," he says. He keeps his gaze on me for a few seconds.

Then I'm thinking about that kiss in college and how it changed everything. How I wanted to kiss him again but also how cruel it was that I couldn't. The way my heart expanded, and I knew only he could do that. And how, even now, even after all this time has passed, I still want his lips on mine.

I blink when I've gone too far back in my mind and clear my throat. It snaps Giancarlo out of it too, because he goes back to unpacking the bag.

"I was thinking we could do a little brainstorming for Mystery Lover. See what we come up with?" He sets a container of pasta in front of me. The aroma of The Golden Lobster's famous alfredo sauce fills the air. It's yet another thing that sends me slipping and sliding down memory lane.

"Good idea." I open the lid on my pasta, stick my fork in it, and take a bite. "Oh my God," I say, closing my eyes.

"I'm guessing it's good?" Giancarlo says.

"I haven't had this in forever. I forgot how much I love it." I savor the creaminess. When I open my eyes,

Giancarlo is looking at me.

"Yeah, me too."

I swallow. It takes three basic words for him to send my heart spiraling in my chest. I have to get through two weeks near this man. Two. Whole. Weeks.

"Let's lay out what we have," I say, desperate to steer us as far away from dangerous territory as possible. "We have the note and the ornament. We know that Grams and Mystery Lover used to frequent Snapdragon Bakery based on the photo on the wall. Snapdragon was owned by Mystery Lover's family."

"And Mystery Lover's family sold the place to Carmine's family."

"And that's all we have. Maybe we're wasting our time. This was a stupid idea," I say.

Giancarlo covers my hand with his. A tingle zips down my spine. "This is a sweet idea. It's what everyone has always loved about you, Felicity."

"Everyone?"

He brushes his thumb across the top of my hand. "Everyone. You're always thinking of others before you think of yourself."

"I just want Grams to be happy."

"Me too." He hesitates and looks at the floor, then says, "You should be happy too. Are you?" He looks like he's holding his breath.

"Feels like there's more to that question."

He pulls his hand back and runs his fingers through his brown waves. "The other day, when you said to Clay that you might be dating, I assumed you meant you were seeing someone. Does he make you happy?"

My eyes go wide, and my heart stops. Why is he asking, and why is he looking at me like that? Like there's a lot riding on my response.

"It's not like I haven't dated. I was trying to show Clay that maybe his assumptions weren't accurate," I say.

"So you're not seeing anyone?"

I shake my head no, and he lets out a deep breath. He takes a sip of his cream soda.

"Why do you care?" I smack his arm playfully.

"I have and always will care about you."

My smile fades. "Then why haven't we talked since…" I can't bring myself to say it, but he knows exactly what I mean because he nods, then stares up at the ceiling.

"That night. The night of our kiss—"

"This is ridiculous," Clay says, leaning on the door frame to my room.

My stomach drops at the sound of his voice. Not because I'm afraid of what he might have just overheard, but because I'm afraid of what might have almost been said.

I shake off all the nostalgia and say, "What's ridiculous?"

Clay strolls into my room, backward baseball cap and all, and very much the uninvited guest. "Here y'all are, repeating history."

Giancarlo raises an eyebrow.

"I've been out distracting Grams with Christmas shopping all day, and you two didn't have the decency to invite me to your dinner. It's just like old times. You could have at least brought me back some pasta."

I laugh. "Do I need to remind you that it was your idea to be the distraction?"

"What choice did I have? She wouldn't buy it if Gi was suddenly interested in chauffeuring her around, and you were already playing Nancy Drew."

"I was minding my business. No one asked you to assume any roles," I say.

Clay shrugs. "So where are we at?"

I fill Clay in while he eats some of the bread he's stolen from Giancarlo's and my dinner.

When I'm done, he says, "I have an idea."

Giancarlo and I stare back at him.

"Hello? Ms. Nettie."

We all smile at each other.

"Grams is hosting her ugly Christmas sweater party tomorrow. You can see if Ms. Nettie knows anything about Mystery Lover."

My phone buzzes next to me. When I pick it up and

flip it over, there's a text from a number I don't recognize. Giancarlo and Clay give me a curious look, and I tap to open the text.

> **Carmine:** *Hey, Felicity. It's Carmine. Wish I had better news, but my parents don't know who is in the photos. They kept them up to honor the legacy of the bakery, but they never knew who was in them. They did remember the last name of the family though: Bianchi.*

I show the text to Clay and Giancarlo.

"Now we're getting somewhere," Clays says.

It's something, but it's not enough. All I can do is keep hoping we get enough information to find Mystery Lover by Christmas.

The sweet smell of rum-soaked cherries, currants, and raisins fill the air while I'm trying to do my research the following day. My mouth waters for the final product: black cake. I'm trying to concentrate on the screen and the fact that there are fifty estimated people in the northern US with the name Bianchi, but the scent is too powerful. I'm not going to get anywhere right now without more information, so I close the laptop and go downstairs. Grams is in the kitchen, blasting parang music.

When she sees me, she lifts her flour-covered hands in the air and swings her hips to the rhythm of the music. She's been this way ever since I can remember. She and Granddad used to dance around the kitchen on just about any occasion. They both loved music. It's still hard to believe she loved another man before Granddad. She must feel conflicted, and maybe that's part of why she doesn't want to dredge up the past. My mind goes in a million different directions. Am I doing the right thing by tracking Mystery Lover down? And am I doing the right thing in my own love life?

"Something on your mind?" Grams asks.

I blink. I hadn't realized she stopped dancing. Now she's standing in front of me, wiping her hands on her Christmas tree apron and staring at me.

"Me? Oh no." I divert my eyes away from hers. Grams has always been good at reading me, a skill she also passed down to my mother.

"Uh-huh." Grams turns back to the kitchen island and starts mixing another batch of cake batter. "For the record, I know you better than that," she says.

I take a seat on one of the bar stools. "How did you know you were in love?" I ask her.

She lifts her gaze and glares at me.

"With Granddad," I quickly correct. Her glare is

confirmation that she assumed I was talking about Mystery Lover.

Her expression softens. "He annoyed me at first," she says, unable to resist a smile.

"Really?" I ask.

"Yeah. Everywhere I turned, he was there. Then he kept showing up to the restaurant where I worked." She shakes her head. "I'd sworn off relationships, *love*. I hadn't planned on falling for anyone ever again."

"But he won you over." I pop a raisin in my mouth.

"Yeah. I tried my hardest to ignore it. I really did. But he was persistent. And then things changed. We got closer when my mom died. He was really there for me. It made me realize that, no matter what, he'd just keep showing up. He wasn't going anywhere. Turned out, that was what I wanted. Someone who wasn't going to leave me."

"And he made you happy?" My mind flashes back to my conversation with Giancarlo. He asked if the imaginary guy he thought I was dating made me happy. Did I want someone who made me feel happy? Yes. But also, was I truly happy at this very moment? Did the choices I made to get me to this point in my life actually *make* me happy? Until Giancarlo asked that question last night, I thought they had.

"Of course. And we have a beautiful family to prove

it." She reaches across the island and taps the back of my hand.

"True," I say, my head still swirling with questions.

"Why all the deep questions?" Grams asks.

I sigh.

"There's that long face again. It's Christmas! 'Tis the season for joy, remember?"

"I know. But it's just a weird Christmas. Mom and Dad aren't here, and—"

"You weren't expecting that old ghost of Christmas past?" Grams starts buttering a baking dish.

"I have no idea what you mean."

"You can deny it all you want. But I have eyes."

I shake my head.

"Is that why you're in your feelings? Maybe there's someone here that you thought you'd forgotten and now you remember *things*?"

I stay quiet.

Grams clears her throat. "You're much younger than I am. You still have time to finish what you started. Come on, help me take these cakes out of the oven so I can put the new ones in. Still lots to do before my ugly Christmas sweater party starts."

I put another raisin in my mouth. The thing is, sometimes when you finish what you start, it also means things end for good.

GIANCARLO

I make one last-ditch effort to sketch something for the mayor's mural, but my brain is too flooded with thoughts—mostly thoughts of Felicity. I've been functioning all this time just fine, and now I've been home for five days and my heart has gone haywire. And it's not like I haven't kept up with her on social media. But pictures online don't have the same energy. And Felicity has always carried a different energy. Or maybe it's just that it feels distinct to me because I've never felt it from anyone else. When I'm in her presence, there's a red carpet my heart rolls out just for her.

I toss my pencil in frustration and close my

sketchbook. I have to figure something out—and quick. Otherwise, this might be the first gig I get fired from. I pick up the ugly sweater I bought earlier from the chair in the corner of the room and pull it over my head. Mrs. James's party is going to start soon. Growing up, it was a tradition I looked forward to. It was just me and my dad for most of my life, and he wasn't big on traditions. He honestly didn't have time for them, really. But coming here and spending time with the James family, especially Felicity, always made me feel at home. I'm still jealous of the connection they have to family and culture—something that left with my mom.

Wonder what she's up to now.

The calypso music booms from downstairs, the official signal that the party has started. I open my door and step out into the hall, and Felicity is passing my door. She stops when she sees me.

"Nice sweater," she says. She eyes the two cats in Santa hats on the front, no doubt reading the text: *Meowy Christmas*. "It's really the cat's pajamas."

I laugh. Hers is covered in tiny red and green pom-poms and tinsel. I touch the gold tinsel sticking out near her shoulder. "You too. I see you've relocated to Tinsel Town."

More laughter. Even in the ugliest of sweaters, she still takes my breath away. I could try, and maybe I'd have to for the rest of my life, but I'll never not want her. If she were mine, I'd pull her close, push the stray curls out of her face, and kiss her in a stolen moment. Then I'd spend the whole party thinking about how we had that moment before and how it was just for us. She looks up at me, and for a second, I think she can read my mind.

"Should we head down?" she asks.

"Yeah." I want to say more, like I have on so many other occasions, but then I remember that very bold line and how we each have our respective sides. But what happens if you want what's on the *other* side?

I follow Felicity down the steps. A few of Felicity and Clay's family members are already downstairs, and Mrs. James is laughing as she opens the front door to let someone else in. It's already pretty loud with the people here and the Trinidadian Christmas music, but it doesn't bother me at all. What it does remind me of is how many quiet Christmases I've had over the last few years. It's nice to be around people, especially people who feel like family. Once we reach the bottom of the stairs, various people stop to greet Felicity. Clay is already in the kitchen when we finally get there, filling up a mini bucket with ice.

He smiles at Felicity and me when we enter. "Most hideous sweater award goes to Felicity." He laughs.

Felicity punches his arm. "Only you would try to

insult my ugly sweater at an ugly sweater party," she says.

"Ow!" Clay shouts dramatically.

"You deserve it," Felicity says.

"You know I'm just messing with you, sis." He pulls Felicity into a bear hug, and she smiles.

Mrs. James pops her head in the entryway to the kitchen. "What are you all doing in here? Clay, the ice is melting. Get out here and stop horsing around with your sister." She disappears.

Clay rolls his eyes. "Duty calls. But in the meantime, I'll try to keep her mostly busy. Ms. Nettie just walked in."

If there's a human being who could be a living, breathing definition of Christmas, it's Ms. Nettie. She removes her coat to reveal a sweater even uglier than Felicity's. It's got green tinsel in the shape of Christmas trees, tiny candy-cane-stripe bows, miniature multicolored ornaments, and fairy lights. In addition to the sweater, she's wearing glittery silver reindeer antlers, bright-green tights, and elf-like shoes.

Felicity leans close to me and whispers, "I can't decide if she's an elf or a reindeer."

I chuckle. "What, you haven't heard of this new hybrid kind of Christmas fan? All the cool kids are half elf, half reindeer."

Felicity laughs. I want that sound on a record to listen to on repeat.

"Grams just walked away. Be my wingman?" she says, searching my eyes.

"Always," I say.

She squeezes my arm, and we set off in the Reindeer-Elf's direction.

Felicity places a hand on Ms. Nettie's shoulder. "Ms. Nettie, hi!"

Ms. Nettie spins around and looks Felicity up and down over her thick, red-framed glasses. "Felicity James!" She throws her arms around Felicity. "You look so good, my dear. And it's so good to have you home."

Then her eyes land on me.

"Hi, Ms. Nettie."

Ms. Nettie adjusts her glasses. "Oh, I don't believe this. Is that you, Giancarlo? Who is this handsome man? We haven't seen you in ages!" She pulls me into the same tight hug she just gave Felicity. When she finally lets me go, she offers the two of us a sly smile. "Oh, please tell me the two of you have finally gotten together." She winks.

I rub the back of my neck as Felicity and I glance at each other.

"Uh, well..." I start.

"We actually didn't know we'd see each other this Christmas," Felicity says. She keeps her eyes on Ms. Nettie.

We are very much not together, but I can't help but feel the weight of disappointment, like an anchor on a string, sinking straight down to the pit of my stomach. We've only been here a few days, and it's the hundredth reminder that she's not mine and never will be. This is why I stopped coming home for Christmas. Too many reminders I don't need.

I half-smile.

"When are you two going to get it together? It's been years of—"

"Ms. Nettie, we were hoping you might be able to help us with something," I say, stopping the wreck this train is headed for.

She adjusts her antlers and says, "What's that, dear?"

"I was chatting with Grams the other day, and she was telling me about the first time she fell in love."

"Oh? She told you that story?"

"Yup. I found the ornament and the letter while we were decorating." Felicity flashes her best smile.

Ms. Nettie gets all serious. "Enzo was something special. She was wild about him. And he was wild about her. Hard to believe things ended the way they did." Ms. Nettie shakes her head.

"Maybe it's not too late for them to find each other again," I say.

Ms. Nettie shakes her head again. "Don't think so. Hazel never heard from him again. No one really knows where he is. Plus, the way he broke your Grams's heart, I don't know that she would forgive him."

"But she might," Felicity says.

"I never say never." Ms. Nettie winks and leans in closer to us. "And just between us, I always thought he was the greatest love of her life. But what are you gonna do? You have to move on after waiting for so long."

"So Grams waited for him after he left?" Felicity asks.

"Yup. She couldn't move on for a while. Then one day, she just carried on. And your granddad was a wonderful man, of course."

"He was," Felicity says. I can see the wheels of her mind turning.

"I'll see you two later. I want to make sure I get some of your Grams's black cake before it's gone!" She dashes off, her antlers slipping a bit to one side.

Felicity looks at me and points up. I nod and follow her lead back up the stairs to the hallway.

"Now we have his whole name! Enzo Bianchi," she says as soon as we're alone. She's pacing back and forth now. It makes me happy to see her happy. She stops and turns to face me, the curved lines of her lips turning into a straight line.

"What's wrong?" I ask.

"It's something Ms. Nettie said." She bites her bottom lip. "She mentioned that Grams was hurt and upset. What if we find this guy and he agrees to surprise

Grams, but then Grams is upset? She already insisted that I not poke around her *business*." She uses air quotes for that last word.

I also had this thought when she first started this mission. "What's your gut say?"

"My gut tells me this is the right thing to do. I can't explain it. But I felt it ever since I confronted Grams about the ornament I found in the attic."

"Okay, let's just say your Grams gets mad. Do you think she'd eventually forgive you?"

She takes a long moment to think about that. "To be honest, I don't know. But I also can't picture her never talking to me again."

"I think if it's a gut feeling, then it's probably worth the chance," I say, looking into her eyes. And maybe I need to take my own advice on that.

"You're right," she says, her eyes never leaving mine. "Thanks."

I push her brown curls out of her face. "You bet."

She sucks in a breath and immediately takes a step away from me. "We should probably get back to the party. I don't want Grams to start asking where we are."

She hurries down the steps before I have a chance to say anything. I don't blame her for running. It's what I did when I ghosted her all those years ago. It's what I've done for years. It doesn't matter that I did it because I didn't know how to handle being near her and staying *just* friends—our friendship didn't deserve that. Felicity didn't deserve that. When you run, though, you eventually have to stop. And maybe that means it's time to finish what I started.

FELICITY

After many hours of internet searches through a million sites and several phone calls, we've finally narrowed the list down to three Enzo Bianchis. One in New York City, one in Portland, Oregon, and one in Lake Margaret, another small town about six hours from Wedgefield.

I rub my temples. "They're all over the place." I'm sitting cross-legged on my bed, leaning back on the headboard.

Giancarlo is on the floor with my laptop on his lap. "And any of these guys could be him. We just need to think harder to find ways we can rule these out."

I throw up my hands. "We've called them all and asked questions. One guy hung up on us, and the other two won't pick up."

"Something tells me one of those two we can't get a hold of might be who we're looking for."

I sit up. "You think Enzo might be upset with Grams in the same way she's upset with him?"

Giancarlo shrugs. "I don't know. But maybe. We don't know all the details of what went down. But that's a possibility. Maybe he's living his life and doesn't want the past disturbing it."

"Grams certainly doesn't," I say. "Or at least she thinks she doesn't."

"Can I ask you something?" Giancarlo studies the floor for a second, then folds his arms over his broad chest.

I nod.

"What made you think your Grams would want this but not admit it?"

I swallow. The truth is, I can't be one hundred percent sure this is what Grams wants. I only know the feeling I got when she finally caved and gave me a handful of details. "First, when she finally admitted to this mystery lover, her face lit up, even if it was only for a second. Then I thought about me."

"You?" He unfolds his arms and places them flat on the floor on either side of him.

"Yeah. I asked myself if I would want to miss out on the love of my life. The answer was no." I can't bring myself to look at him after the last sentence.

He's quiet at first, then he says, "Me too."

"Have you, um…come close to that? Finding the love of your life, I mean. It's been a while since we checked in." I'm not supposed to be jealous, but I almost don't want to know the answer. If he's come close with another woman, that means someone else has been getting to know all the parts that he only showed to me. And even though he's not mine, I don't like it. I want to be the only one who gets those parts of him.

He steadies his gaze on me. "It has been a while, hasn't it? The last time I checked, you were about to go on a first date with Paul Winfrey."

I get quiet because the period of time he's referring to is supposed to be one we locked away—one I try not to think about because I decided I wasn't going to relive that kiss anymore. I did that so many times after it happened. Bringing it up now is punishment.

Giancarlo's eyes widen when he realizes why I've become quiet, and then we both don't say anything for a bit.

He circles back to my question. "You know, I've dated a little over the last few years, but I've only ever come close to the real thing once."

The words split my heart, and I feel every jagged edge of the zigzag ridges. There *has* been someone else. "Oh. So you have a girlfriend?" I can't even stop myself from asking the question. If only I'd think for two seconds, I'd save myself from further torture. But I can't take it back now.

He shakes his head. "Nope. My schedule's a little hectic with all the traveling, and it's kind of complicated with the person I want."

This moment might just swallow me whole. "Right," I say. I don't want to hear any more. I can't hear any more. It's like the room is running out of oxygen. This is why I didn't fight him when he abandoned our friendship. I can't handle discussions about other women. I change the subject. We're running out of time to find Mystery Lover, anyway. "Should we try calling our three guys again?"

I make it my mission to avoid those sepia eyes demanding exploration.

His eyebrows knit together, and if I didn't know better, I would think there might be some hurt in there. I look away too quickly to tell for sure, though. We probably both hurt each other back then. The difference between him and me is that he's moved on. Whatever's been showing up between us on this trip is probably just nostalgia. We were close after all.

"Yeah. Let's give it another shot," Giancarlo says, his

deep, rich voice now lackluster.

I pick up my phone and try one of the numbers again, grateful for somewhere other than Giancarlo to put my attention. The sooner we find Mystery Lover, the sooner we can get back to our regularly scheduled lives.

An hour later, we've narrowed the three Enzos down to two. I let out a long sigh when I hang up the phone.

"Another one bites the dust," I say, stretching. "Can't believe it took us this long to figure out that all we had to do was ask if they went to Wedgefield High. Now, if we could just get the other two to pick up the phone."

"Better late than never, and they'll pick up eventually." Giancarlo crosses the Enzo from Portland—the same one that initially hung up on us—off the list.

That gets me thinking. "But what if they don't? It doesn't matter how many times someone calls me, if it's an unknown number, I never pick it up."

Giancarlo laughs. "I remember."

I smirk because I know the exact memory he's thinking of.

"Imagine applying for a summer internship and repeatedly not answering the same unknown number. I can't believe it never occurred to you that it might be them," he says, another laugh escapes him.

I can't help but laugh too. "They should have left a message!"

"They eventually did...except you never check messages." He will not stop laughing now.

I shrug. "Whatever. Some jobs aren't meant to be. I turned out just fine without it."

Giancarlo checks his phone. "Fair point," he says, distracted by whatever is on his screen. Maybe it's the one who he thinks things are complicated with?

"You know, if you need to take a break and do what you have to do, that's totally fine. I can keep trying to get a hold of the last two." I try to keep my voice cool, but inside, everything's still crashing down as I remember the uncomfortable conversation we just had before continuing the Enzo search.

He looks up from his phone, one of his brown waves falling close to his eyes. "There's nothing to take care of that isn't in this room," he says.

My heart lurches. Him saying things like that is what makes me doubt my decisions. I move on so my brain doesn't latch onto that comment. "It really would be okay. We probably need a break. I promised Grams I'd go wrap gifts for the children's hospital. Plus, I want to take all the ornaments I made over."

"I didn't know she still did that. Is it still at the

community center?"

"Every year," I say.

He smiles. "And you made ornaments? Do you even sleep?"

"I do it every year. I make them throughout the year since I have access to the kiln at Muralo. It's nice for them to have a Christmas tradition of their own. And they can take it with them."

He doesn't say anything for a few seconds, just studies me like he's trying to figure something out. "See what I mean? You're always thinking about what others need. I've always liked that about you."

I blush. It's yet another thing to give me false hope.

"Can I come?" he asks.

I stand up. "Yeah, but don't you have things to do, people to respond to?"

"It can wait." Giancarlo stands up too, and now we're standing chest to chest, the space between us only a sliver. "I really want to help."

I press my lips together, then say, "Okay." I hurry up and turn around to leave, but he catches my wrist. The touch is the tipping point for the ripple that follows. I face him again.

"Are you okay?" he asks.

"Fine," I say.

"I know it's been a while, but I know you well enough to

know that you're not fine whenever you use the word fine."

I look down, and he's still holding my hand. What am I supposed to say? I can't tell him I'm jealous that he just admitted he's only come close to being in love once, and it's with someone else. Of course I'd known that was a possibility, but him saying it out loud makes it a very real thing. It's stupid for me to hope we could be anything more than friends.

I pull my hand away. I have to get out of this room. "Don't worry about me. We probably need to get going. Grams is probably already at the center, and I don't want to be late." And then I hurry out of the room before he has the chance to stop me again. It's probably the easy way out, but it's the only thing I can think to do. My willpower is already running thin. Turns out, when you're trying to get the rough draft of the story right, it might not go the way you want it to. You'll have to determine if there's a way to sort out the story—or scrap it entirely.

GIANCARLO

The entire ride over to the Wedgefield Community Center is a little awkward. Our rideshare drops us off on the sidewalk—Felicity with a rolling cart full of her ornaments. Before we head inside, I tug Felicity's hand for the second time that day. I need to talk to her before we go inside, but to be honest, I'd find a million excuses to touch her.

She doesn't turn around at first, which puzzles me. She's been acting so weird since our Enzo internet search.

"Are you okay? Tell me for real." I look into her eyes. Behind all that beauty, there's something wrong.

She meets my eye, but it's half a second before she's

looking into the distance, anywhere but at me. "I already told you, I'm fine."

"It just feels like something's off. I thought we were—" I pause because I have to be careful with my words. No matter how much I want to cross the line, I'm not supposed to.

"Thought we were what?" she says, searching my eyes.

"I thought we were having a good time," I say. I don't say what I really want to say, which is that I thought we were having a moment. I've only been back home a few days, but to me, we keep entering these slivers of time where I think she feels what I feel. I don't say how there's this thing between us, but there's also always an elephant in the room named Clay—and quite literally, at that.

"We are." She doesn't shake me off, just softens. "I think we should get in there, though. They're waiting for us, and they could probably use the help."

She gives my hand a squeeze before letting go. It gives me hope—hope I probably shouldn't have—but also, I can't quite read her either.

I follow her up the plastic candy cane-lined pathway to the front door of the center. She pulls open the heavy tan door with a giant wreath on it.

As soon as we enter, we bump into Clay, who's exiting with a big box of already wrapped toys.

He smiles when he sees us.

"Need any help with that?" I nod to the box his arms are wrapped around.

"Nah, I'm good. Loading up the van, and it's just outside." He motions to Felicity's cart of ornaments. "I can take those too if you want to leave them right here."

"Okay, thanks." Felicity rolls it to the wall next to us.

Clay glances around and shifts the box he's carrying off to the side so he can lean in closer, his eyes barely visible under his black baseball cap. "Any luck?"

Felicity's warm expression fades. "Still don't have a pulse on the official Enzo, but we narrowed it down to two."

"Well, that's progress, sis," Clay says.

"It is. I'm just getting worried about the time." She lets out a deep breath.

"You know what Grams always says: keep the faith."

She tries to smile, but it's a weak one.

"There you two are," Mrs. James says. Her voice booms from the far end of the space.

Clay glances over his shoulder. "That's my cue. Gotta go." He jets off as Grams makes her way over to us.

Felicity kisses Mrs. James on the cheek. "Sorry we're late, Grams. We got held up...uh, running a few errands." She glances at me, and I hope my eyes don't give away the surprise from her almost spilling the beans.

Mrs. James pats my arm and gives me a warm smile. "I didn't know you were coming, Giancarlo."

"When Felicity mentioned she was coming here, I had to help too," I say.

"You're just as sweet now as you were as a little gentleman." Mrs. James pinches my cheek. "Okay, I've got a table right over there for the two of you." She leads us across the room. We move through rows of folding tables with volunteers wrapping gifts. The sound of tearing paper, Scotch tape, and chatter fill the air.

Once we're standing in front of a table, Mrs. James points. "You two can sit here. The tall box next to this table has all the gifts you'll have to wrap. Do your best to make them look nice. We want the kids to enjoy the experience as much as possible."

I run my fingers through my hair. I did sort of forget that I'd need to do a decent job wrapping these gifts. When I look over at Felicity, she's got her hand over her mouth, trying to hide a smile. She remembers everything about me.

"I gotta go. Some more volunteers just walked in," Mrs. James says.

"What are you laughing at?" I say.

"I feel bad for the kids who are going to get the gifts you wrap." She lets her hand drop to her stomach as she laughs, no longer trying to cover that captivating smile. She might be laughing at me, but I couldn't care less if it means getting even a glimpse of her happiness.

"Hey, my wrapping isn't so bad. I've improved," I say.

"Really?" She folds her arms across her chest and raises an eyebrow.

I fold my arms for a second and stare back, challenging her. Then I let them fall to my sides. "No. But I could be better now. A lot of time has passed."

She laughs, and the two of us go to the box wrapped in Christmas tree paper next to our table. Our hands touch as we reach in to grab a toy. There it is again. This thing that bounces like charged up atoms between us. It happens every time we share a memory, every time we make eye contact, every time we touch. I can't be imagining it.

She pulls her hand back. "You can grab yours first."

We settle into our seats, and I flip over the Transformers toy I picked. Maybe I'm secretly hoping for wrapping instructions.

"I think you might be in over your head," Felicity says, rolling her wrapping paper out on her side of the table. "Come stand next to me. We can do it together."

She doesn't have to ask me twice. No way I'm turning down another chance to be near her.

"Try rolling out the wrapping paper, then placing the gift on top. That way you can measure how much you need to cover the whole thing."

I follow her lead as she takes me through all the steps

of gift wrapping. "You're such a pro at this." I watch how she carefully folds the pieces of paper neatly over the doll box she's wrapping.

"Well, I've had some practice. Grams and Granddad always loved this tradition," she says.

"I didn't have very many presents to wrap." I think back to Dad and how he was always working. "Christmas reminded Dad of Mom, so…"

"And how do you feel about Christmas? Does it remind you of your mom?"

"The memories are foggy. But it does a little. One of the only clear memories I have of her is making Italian Christmas cookies. She loved baking at Christmastime."

I reach for the tape, and Felicity places her hand on my wrist. It does absolutely nothing for the already unhealthy longing for her I've been trying to fight off. I look down at where her hand is then back at her. She doesn't let up.

"I'm sorry you had to go through that."

"I was lucky to have a remarkable friend to help me get through it."

Her eyelids flutter, caught in the riptide of a blush.

"It's why I wanted to come here with you today." I'm not going to tell her the part about me taking every chance I can to get next to her. That's half of it. I tell her the other half instead. "Maybe there's a kid like me who needs something special. I was lucky. At least I had a dad. Our relationship was complicated, but at least he stuck around. And, deep down, I know he loves me. He just has a hard time showing love after being burned."

"Unpopular opinion, but maybe your mom loves you too," she says.

I shake my head. "She's got a funny way of showing it."

"Maybe she's scared." Her thumb brushes against the underside of my wrist and then settles again.

"Maybe. But did she think about how scared I was back then. I—"

"Needed her?" Felicity finishes.

I nod.

"Do you think you could forgive her? You might not be able to have the ideal kind of relationship, but what if she's hurting the way you are?"

"Who says I'm hurting?" I say with all the stubbornness I can add.

She squeezes my wrist and presses her lips together. Once again, she knows exactly how to read me.

"You believe Grams and Mystery Lover deserve a second chance, right?"

"You know I do."

"Just checking. They might not be the only ones," she says.

She squeezes my hand one more time before picking

up the scissors to cut more wrapping paper.

I've never liked talking about my mom, but Felicity has always been the only one to get me to do it. I haven't talked about Mom in years. The memory of her blurred as more time passed, and I'd talked myself into thinking it was for the best. But now, Felicity has me wondering if that was truth, or if that was something I made up and called truth.

My phone buzzes in my coat pocket, and I tense because I can feel exactly who it is. I look over at Felicity, and she has the same look on her face that she did earlier during the Enzo search. Her lips stretch into a straight line as I try to search her eyes to figure it out. So many different emotions. Disappointment? Longing? Curiosity?

"Go ahead and grab it. I'm out of wrapping paper, and I'm gonna go find Grams to see if she can get me more."

I'm about to tell her I don't have to get it, but she's already racing down the rows of tables. Any faster and she'd be literally running. I wrinkle my brows and turn back to my phone. Might as well answer it now.

When I tap the screen, there's a message from Riley, as expected.

> **Riley:** *Starting to wonder why you're not back here.*

> **Giancarlo:** *I just need a little more time.*

I watch the screen as the text bubbles move back and forth. Riley's frustration is almost palpable. She's been pretty calm overall, but I can tell she's starting to lose patience with me. It's threaded into her every word.

> **Riley:** *With all due respect, Mr. Westbrook, we've given you a lot of time already.*

> **Giancarlo:** *I know.*

And they have, but it doesn't change the fact that I've still got nothing. Going back to Marvelwest wouldn't mean that I'd be magically inspired. I'd just be in the same boat. When she doesn't answer, I throw in another text for good measure.

> **Giancarlo:** *I really appreciate your patience. I won't let you or the mayor down.*

> **Riley:** *Remember, I stuck my neck out for you to take the time off. And it was only supposed to be a couple days.*

Not to mention she got Mayor Ortiz to agree to a New Year's mural instead of a Christmas one. But obviously, I'm not going to remind her of that.

> **Giancarlo:** *You have my word.*

> **Riley:** *Okay...*

I don't blame her for losing faith. Tonight, it's just me, my sketchbook, and maybe some of Mrs. James's leftover black cake—if Clay hasn't gotten to it first. Those thoughts leave my mind immediately when I look up and see Felicity laughing with a guy I don't recognize on the other side of the room. Whatever he's saying must be really freaking funny because Felicity throws her head back, then places a hand on his arm—and I don't like it.

I jump to my feet and stick my hands in my pocket, my eyes glued to them as they huddle over Felicity's phone. Before I can stop myself, I march over, everything and everyone else in the room disappearing.

"Who's this?" I say once I'm standing in front of them.

Now both Felicity and whoever this is, are looking up at me. He's about my height and wearing a long-sleeve shirt with a snowman on the front. It doesn't get past me that they're still huddled pretty close with Felicity's phone still between them in the palm of her hand. Felicity is looking at me like she's trying to solve a puzzle, and Mr. Snowman is looking at me half confused, half challenging.

I take a step closer to Felicity. "Who's your friend, Felicity?" Emphasis on friend.

Felicity doesn't ease up on the puzzled expression,

just tilts her head to the side. She glances back at Mr. Snowman and says, "This is Andrew."

"What's up, man?" Mr. Snowman—Andrew—extends his hand, and when I shake it, I make sure it's firm.

"Nice to meet you," I say even though it absolutely isn't.

Andrew glances back and forth from me to Felicity as we both stare at each other. Andrew clears his throat. "So, how do you two know each other?"

I finally shift my attention back to Andrew. "We're... old friends." Then it hits me that I have to call her friend, and I hate it. I don't want her to be my friend. I want more, and I always have. It would have been so different if I kept living my life and never had to see her again, but I came home, and now I'm making a fool of myself because, straight up? I'm jealous.

"You cool?" Andrew asks.

I snap back to reality, realizing I just had a full-on life epiphany in my head, and a total stranger got to witness it. "It was nice to meet you, Allen. Excuse me."

"It's Andrew," I hear over my shoulder.

But I'm too busy racing to the exit. I don't even grab my coat. I step outside into the cold, hoping it will shock some sense into me. I thought I had scrubbed Felicity out of my system. I'm falling for her again—I never stopped.

"Giancarlo?" I hear her voice behind me.

I close my eyes, still spinning from my realization.

Felicity appears before me. "Are you sick?"

Maybe, but not in the way she thinks. She doesn't even know she's undone me. "I'm fine." Nothing to see here.

"Like you said to me earlier, I know when you're not fine." She folds her arms over her chest.

I take a deep breath, but I don't say anything. What am I supposed to say? Hey, I literally cannot stop thinking about you, and even though I've tried to fall out of love with you, it won't work?

"What exactly was that back there?"

A few people pass us outside the center.

"What was what?"

The same confused look from earlier returns to her face. "For starters, you were pretty rude to Andrew. I mean, even calling him by the wrong name? That's not like you at all, Giancarlo."

"Well, you're not wrong," I mumble.

She takes a step closer to me, closing the distance between us. And before I know it, her arms are around my neck, pulling me close to her. That sweet rosy scent fills my head and makes me dizzy. I wrap my hands around her waist, the thought again coming to me that there's no home like her, and there never will be.

"Talk to me," she whispers.

I don't say anything at first, just press my forehead to hers. We both stand in the cold, eyes closed. "I don't know if I can say it out loud yet."

"Okay." She's breathless and takes a step back.

Our eyes don't seem to want to leave each other.

"I'm here to listen when you're ready."

I nod. She makes her way back to the door. And then it's just me, my thunderbolt secret, and the faint smell of rose.

FELICITY

In the baking aisle of the Wedgefield Supermarket, I stand still, staring at shelves with sacks of flour. My mind keeps replaying the moment yesterday with Giancarlo outside of the Wedgefield Community Center. He can make anything feel romantic, even a simple hug. It takes me back to when we were sixteen and he'd text me after his shift at The Golden Lobster that he was bringing me pasta. Everyone else in the world would have just said, so what? Doesn't have to mean anything. It's a pretty basic thing for someone to bring you food. But to me, it meant everything.

And then there was the moment before that with

Andrew. Giancarlo was acting so strange, not like himself at all. I thought I was making it up until he stormed out of the center. I'd been watching the way his eyes held something mystifying. It was half angry, half authoritative. The whole time, only one question revolved in my mind: *Is he jealous?*

I pick up one of the bags of flour and toss it in the cart. As I make my way around the store to gather the rest of my baking supplies, I can't think of anything else. It feels like the unfinished draft of us somehow got out of that locked drawer. To finish or not to finish, that is the revived question.

Back at Grams's house, I spread out all the ingredients I bought on the kitchen island and put the recipe I printed out next to the items. I reach for one of Grams's aprons and slip it over my head, then prep everything the way they would on one of those TV baking shows. Hopefully, this plan doesn't backfire. I send a text to Giancarlo.

Felicity: Need a break?

Giancarlo: *You read my mind. What are you thinking?*

Felicity: *Come downstairs.* ☺

Giancarlo: *Your wish is always my command.* ☺

In less than a minute, he's entering the kitchen. It's hard not to stare at his dark, messy hair and the charcoal-gray sweats he's wearing. You could put him in a tin-foil suit and he'd still pull it off. He'd still make my heart accelerate.

His eyes drop to the counter, and he narrows them, then smiles when he shifts his attention back to me. "What's all this?"

I love that smile. "Okay, so hear me out."

"Okay..."

"Hopefully, you don't think I'm overstepping, but I just thought maybe we could make the Italian cookies your mom used to make. You always said you didn't know much about your Italian roots, and I thought maybe we could learn about it together. I looked up a recipe and—" It registers that I'm rambling, and when I stop to finally look at him, I can't quite read his expression.

I pick up the printout of the recipe so I don't have to look at him and say, "I'm overstepping. I'm sorry. I don't know what I was thinking—"

"Felicity," Giancarlo says. "Have I told you lately how wonderful you are?"

My heart doesn't even hesitate. It takes off sprinting in my chest without giving me a say. I'm quiet because I wasn't expecting him to say that.

He holds my gaze, then reaches for my free hand,

slowly bringing it close to his lips. He holds it suspended there, his thumb brushing over the inside of my wrist, his breath warm against my skin. He doesn't take his eyes off me, and maybe he's asking me if I want him to stop without actually asking me. When I say nothing, he brings his lips to my wrist. The subtle touch exposes a secret my heart has been keeping.

But he's not mine.

I clear my throat, then slowly pull my hand away. "We should get started." When I take the chance to glance at him, his hand is still frozen in place.

He finally drops it, then says, "Yeah."

We're both quiet for a few minutes, and I busy myself dumping the ingredients into a bowl. Meanwhile, my mess of a mind tries to push emotions aside and think of *anything* else to say.

"So how's the mural sketching coming?"

"It wasn't going that great, honestly," Giancarlo says.

"And now?" I ask, pulling a few ingredients closer to me.

"After the wrapping event, let's just say I'm inspired." His smile threatens to unravel me again.

I pick up the sugar instead of losing myself in the way he makes me feel. "That's good, right?" I hand him the printout for the glaze.

"It is."

"I'll work on the dough while you work on the glaze?"

He nods.

"Does this bring back any weird memories?" I ask as I'm stirring the ingredients in the bowl.

"The thing is, I don't remember much. I just remember the aftermath. The way Dad was never the same. Which also meant our relationship was never the same. I'm not sure what I would have done if it weren't for your family."

"I'm glad we could be there for you," I say.

"Me too."

"Do you think you can at least work on repairing the relationship with either of them?"

"Good question." He pauses his whisking and stares straight ahead. "I don't know. Dad and I talk, but we just don't have that warm, fuzzy, father-son thing going on. And I only hear from Mom periodically. I kind of get the feeling she doesn't really want to have a better relationship."

"Have you asked her?"

He's quiet for a second. "I have not."

"Maybe you should."

"It just feels too…late," he says.

"It's never too late," I say. I should listen to my own words on that one. "You know what? It's Christmas. Baking was supposed to be fun. Tell me something happy about your mom baking these."

He gives a half smile. "You know why she started making these?"

I shake my head. "I don't think you've ever told me."

"I was a picky eater. And once upon a time, there were only five things on the list of foods I would eat. Naturally, Mom would make some of my grandmother's old recipes. And, well, the Christmas cookies were part of her childhood tradition. The first time she made them, she caught me sitting on the kitchen floor, eating from the tin one night."

I laugh. "What!"

"Yup. I made a mess too. There were crumbs scattered everywhere. But she didn't even get mad. She just smiled, let me finish the cookie in my hand, cleaned up, and put me back to sleep."

"That's sweet," I say.

He nods. "I guess it was."

"Maybe one day you can go to Italy and visit her. And who knows? Maybe you'll meet family and learn more about who you are," I say.

"Maybe," he says, but I can tell the idea makes him uncomfortable.

"I've always wanted to visit. You should go," I say.

"Only if you come with me."

"You don't need me." I finish mixing the dough.

"I do need you, Felicity James. And I should have told you that instead of letting our friendship fizzle out."

I accidentally knock over the sugar, the jar falling over on its side. Thank God it doesn't break. Grams would kill me for breaking her precious Fitz and Floyd canister. I hurry over to where the paper towels are over the sink and unroll a bunch in my hands. I'm trying my hardest to keep myself moving. If I just keep moving, I don't have to look at him. I don't have to concentrate on the way my heart keeps calling for him. I don't have to get lost in those autumn eyes. If I keep moving, my brain won't have to concentrate on what he just said. Because the second he starts needing me is the second I aim to please.

"Felicity—"

My phone buzzes. And never before have I been so thankful to hear that stupid, peppy iPhone ding.

I pick it up and say right away to Giancarlo, "I should check this."

His shoulders deflate, but he nods.

Andrew: *Hey, Felicity! I have some news I think you're going to like!*

Felicity: *Trying not to get ahead of myself! What is it?*

Andrew: *It looks like my family remembered Enzo's family when they had the restaurant next door.*

> **Felicity:** *So do they know why his family left and why they sold the bakery?*

> **Andrew:** *Enzo's dad was sick, and they had to leave to get him better care and be around more family. They moved to Lake Margaret. That's all my family/parents said.*

> **Felicity:** *Andrew, I can't thank you enough!*

> **Andrew:** *Maybe let me take you out for a hot chocolate?* ☺

I lift my gaze and find Giancarlo staring at me. Again, I can't read him. But I do know one thing: another man just asked me out, and my immediate reaction? Giancarlo. Whether I realized it or not, I've learned him by heart. And when you commit something to memory, it doesn't just go away. It remains whether you want it to or not. And now that I'm home and getting to spend time with him like when we were younger, I don't want to lose him. But I don't know how to tell him—and I sure don't know how to avoid ruining my relationship with my brother.

But it's a problem for another time, because right now I need to get back to my bigger mission. I'm not sure what to say to Andrew. The man just gave me the equivalent of several pieces to my puzzle. The least I could do is meet him for hot chocolate. I type in a smiley face, then click my phone off. I put it down, then place both my arms on the counter so they're wide apart.

"What is it?" Giancarlo asks.

"That was Andrew."

Giancarlo presses his lips together and rubs the back of his neck. "And, uh…what did he say?"

"His family remembered the Bianchis." I fill him in on the details.

"So that means we can confirm the one in New York City is out. He's in Lake Margaret. We found him," he says, his lips spreading into a smile.

"Yeah," I say. Before, Enzo felt like some fairytale man from Grams's past, but now he's real.

"So why does your face say sad winter song instead of 'Holly Jolly Christmas'?" he asks.

That gets me to crack a smile. "We don't know for sure that it's him, since we can't get him on the phone. And if it is him, I just remembered my relationship with Grams is on the line too."

"Take a chance, remember?"

I nod. "When did that become our theme song?"

He grins, which only highlights the twinkle in his eye that made me fall for him to begin with. "Maybe it always has been."

GIANCARLO

Maybe it's the warm sugar-butter aroma still hanging in the air from our baking session. Or maybe it's the glow from the warm lights Mrs. James has throughout her entire house. Maybe it's my hometown, where I spent so many nights sharing secrets with the girl I thought I could never have. Maybe it's me being next to her. Whatever it is, it all makes me aware of an ache in my bones that only comes from realizing what you've been missing.

This is what I'm thinking about as we sit in the living room, trying to explain our latest discovery to Clay. They're both sitting across from me, Felicity with her laptop open, and Clay slouched down in his backward baseball cap.

"Look at Nancy Drew coming through," Clay says, draping an arm around Felicity's shoulders. He just walked back in the house after dropping Mrs. James off at Ms. Nettie's. Mrs. James insisted on wrapping some of her presents there because she didn't trust our "prying eyes," according to Clay.

"We still have to make sure this is the right guy."

"True. Sounds like he might be stuck in 1960. Who in this modern world isn't always on their phone?"

"Well, he doesn't know who we are," Felicity says.

Clay pulls out his phone, and after a few taps, holds it up. "I just Googled his name and Lake Margaret. The One Ornament gift shop just popped up. Boom."

"Let me see that." Felicity takes his phone, reading through what's on the screen. "This has to be him. And check out the name of the shop. *The One* Ornament?" She places a hand over her heart. "We can find out everything about him, but it doesn't mean we can get him to take our call."

Clay snaps his fingers, his eyes all of a sudden as bright as the Christmas lights. "I got it."

Felicity and I stare at him while he revels in the suspense. He's always been dramatic.

"I can't believe you two don't see it."

Felicity rolls her eyes. "Out with it, Clay."

He grins. "You go to him, then."

Felicity snorts. "What's in that hot chocolate?" She nods to his cup.

"You got any better ideas?" Clay asks.

I wrinkle my brows. "Lake Margaret is six hours away."

"How we gonna get there, Sherlock?" Felicity says.

"I haven't quite figured that part out yet, my dear Nancy." Clay gives her an amused smile.

"We only have Grams's car here, so that's out. Plus, everything's probably already booked up," I say.

Clay leans back, folding his arms and staring at the floor. After a few moments, he sits up again and leans forward. "What about the train?"

Felicity shakes her head. "First, if everything is booked, then the train probably will be too. And second, are we really going to entertain this conversation?"

"Uh-huh," Clay says. "You can usually find something on the late trains."

"So you want us to get on a night train and travel six hours to get to a man who we don't even know is the mystery lover we're looking for?" I let out a short laugh.

"Like I said, if you two can come up with a better plan, I'm all ears."

"Why don't *you* get on a train, then?" Felicity says.

"We agreed I would keep Grams busy." Clay sticks

out his chest.

Felicity sighs.

"Come on, we've already come this far. No turning back now." Clay shrugs.

"We?" Felicity says.

I forgot how entertaining it is to witness their back and forth.

Clay places a hand on his chest, his mouth forming an *O*. "After all I've done for this cause, Felicity?"

She rolls her eyes again.

Clay laughs. "In all seriousness, you'll be with Giancarlo. He'll take care of you."

My eyes go wide at the mention of my name. Not because I'm surprised, but because it dawns on me that I'd be alone with Felicity. Like, alone-*alone*. No Clay walking in and interrupting. No Mrs. James. No one we know. Just me and her.

Felicity chews on her bottom lip.

"Come on, sis," Clay presses.

Her eyes rise slowly to mine. I offer her a warm smile—one I hope she can feel.

"Okay. For Grams." I can tell she's trying to convince herself this is what's best.

"Atta girl." Clay leans over so he can see her laptop screen. "Now comes the hard part—finding tickets."

The three of us nod collectively.

After several minutes of clicking, tapping, and scrolling, we finally land on something for late the following night.

"I think the 12 AM tomorrow is the best choice. You'll get there at 6 AM. And you'll have the whole day to convince him before you get back on the train at 6 PM," Clay says.

Felicity and I look at each other, then nod. While she's booking the tickets, she asks, "And what are we going to tell Grams?"

Clay rubs his chin. "That's a good question."

"Why don't we tell her the mayor insisted I ride back to do some paperwork, and Felicity went with me? You think she'd buy that?" I ask.

"I think so. I mean, she knows you're just here to regroup, and I've told her that the mayor has been pressing you," Clay says.

Considering Riley and the mayor would rather have me back working on the mural, it does sound like something I might have to do.

Felicity taps on the last key, her computer making a whoosh sound. "Then it's official. I just emailed the tickets to you both."

"Here we go," Clay says.

The next night, while throwing a few things in my backpack, Clay knocks on my door.

"Hey, what's up, man?" I say, tossing my sketchbook in my bag.

Clay leans on the wall, folding his arms across his chest. "Hey."

I glance over my shoulder. "Everything okay?" I ask.

"Yeah. I realized that I kind of just volunteered you for all of this. You know, with helping Felicity and then going with her to Lake Margaret."

"It's cool. We're all friends, right? Besides, I'd love to be part of this for Mrs. James. She was always so warm and welcoming to me growing up. I'll never forget that."

"Well, Grams loves you. She was always asking about you when you stayed away, you know."

I swallow the lump in my throat. I never wanted them to think I didn't want to be around them. It was just hard being around Felicity and knowing she'd never be mine. "I owe her an apology. I didn't mean for so much time to pass. I got caught up trying to make it as an artist."

"You sure that's all?" he asks. This time, he makes eye contact and doesn't let up. Maybe he knows. Maybe I don't care that he knows. All I know is that I want Felicity, and it feels like I need to stop running. But I can't tell Clay before I tell her.

"Yeah, that's all."

He's quiet for a little bit before saying, "Okay. Well, do me a favor?"

"Sure," I say. Again, I wonder if he's going to confront me. Guilt lingers in my chest.

"Look out for her, okay?"

"Always," I say, looking at him straight on.

"You always have, haven't you?" he says. It's barely noticeable, but his eyes narrow a little. He lets out a deep breath, then says, "Thanks, man."

And then he's gone. Meanwhile, I think about all the time I was too much of a coward to say what I wanted. I always told Felicity that I couldn't understand my dad. That he hardly said what he was thinking ever. To this day, he isn't a man of many words. And yet, here I am, doing the same thing. I don't know if there's any hope for him, but I don't want to be like him. And that means telling my truth.

FELICITY

I sit next to Giancarlo inside the train station while we wait to board our train to Lake Margaret. By far, this is one of the wildest things I've ever done, and I have no way of knowing if it will even work out. And if that wasn't enough of a plot twist, I'm getting on a train with the man I've been in denial about loving. Christmas is going well.

Giancarlo turns his head to look at me. "You okay?" he asks.

I nod. "I will be. It's almost midnight. I'm just tired, you know?"

"You know I do." He smirks, then yawns. "That's why

we got one of the sleeper cars, right? You can pass out when we board."

I laugh, but it's more of a nervous one. Because now I'm thinking about being in that tiny little train car with him. At least those cars usually have two beds. My chest tightens, and when I get out of my head, Giancarlo's looking at me, head tilted to the side. "Sorry. I'm just a little on edge."

My hand is on the armrest between us, and he covers it with his. Even though that makes my heart beat faster, somehow, it also makes me feel safe.

He gives it a squeeze. "I don't know a single person on this planet with a heart bigger than yours. Whatever happens, whether your grams gets mad at you, or Enzo refuses to talk to us, your heart is in the right place. And I happen to know that your heart is one of the most wonderful places to be." His thumb brushes the side of my index finger, and inside, everything sparks.

"Thank you," I say, holding his gaze.

His phone beeps again, and now I'm thinking about whoever he's been texting.

He looks at the screen, then pushes it back in his pocket.

"You can get that if you want—if she's someone important, I mean."

He studies my face for a few seconds, then says, "She?"

"We've been friends forever. You taught me how to

kiss, remember? I think you can tell me if you have a girlfriend." There. Now the elephant can run free.

"That was a work email. The mayor's office is anxious for me to finish the mural. Felicity, I don't have a girlfriend. It's kind of hard to have one when you're—"

But the announcer's voice on the speaker overhead interrupts. "Now boarding train 2248 nonstop to Lake Margaret."

Giancarlo stands and slings his backpack over one shoulder. Then he reaches for mine, slinging it over his other shoulder.

"Ready?" he asks.

"Yeah," I say, though it might be the understatement of the century.

Once we find our sleeper car, it's much smaller than I thought. We step through the doors, and Giancarlo slides it closed behind us. I expected it to smell older, like the memories of the thousands of people who have been here, but all that fills the air is a spicy soap scent. He is everywhere without even trying. While Giancarlo sets our bags down on the sliver of space next to the two seats opposite of each other, I take a deep breath. It hasn't even been five minutes, and I'm already wondering how I'm going to survive six hours this close to him. Once this train starts moving, there will be nowhere to run. I turn around to take off my coat, and we both bump into each other, my eyes now level with his chest. I pause before lifting my gaze to his.

Giancarlo laughs. "I guess it's a little tight, huh?"

"Yeah," I say. My cheeks are a firepit. Any second now, the rest of me could burst into flames.

His gaze shifts to the two seats facing each other along the only window of the sleeper car and then up to the panel that opens out to a second bed. "Should I go ahead and set up our beds? I can convert the seats for you, and I'll take the one up top? It's already pretty late, and we're going to be on the road for a while before we make it back home. The more sleep we get now, the better."

"Very true, and that sounds good," I say. We put our coats with our bags, and I can't help but notice the way he looks in his sweats. They're just the right size, and when he moves, every so often his toned muscles peek through. More than anything, I want him to wrap his arms around me.

Giancarlo reaches up and tries to pull down the upper bunk, which doesn't budge. "Uh-oh," he says, continuing to yank the latch.

I try to help him, but no matter how much we push, pull, and prod, it won't budge.

"Now what?" I ask.

He runs his fingers through his hair. "Well, maybe we can call someone to help? Or they can move us to a different sleeper car?"

I shake my head. "It's a full train."

We're both staring at the floor now. The sound of the train whistle fills the air, and the train starts to move.

"It's a tiny bed, but we could share it?" My voice isn't much more than a whisper. We're still facing each other, but it also feels like the car is running out of air, or maybe it's just my lungs. I take a step back from him anyway, though it doesn't put much distance between us.

"You sure you'd be okay with that?" he asks, his voice quieter and seemingly deeper.

"It'll be just like the thousands of nights we spent lying on the same blanket and looking up at stars," I say.

He smiles. "Some of my favorite nights."

"Me too. And we're friends, right?" I ask it, but I hate this question. It's like a math equation I can't solve—one where I'm adding and subtracting what we mean to each other.

He focuses his attention on the floor, and I can tell he's thinking about something. A few seconds go by before he says, "You remember the night we kissed?" He's still not looking at me.

Do I remember? I've spent the last six years trying to forget it. "Of course I remember it."

He laughs, then looks up at me again, dropping the smile. "I lied."

My gut wrenches as my brain skims the memory. "Oh." It's all I can manage to get out as he waits for me to say something.

"I told you that I'd teach you how to kiss so you wouldn't be worried about your first kiss. But..." He pauses, his eyes confirming everything I've ever wanted through his thick, dark lashes. "But I was looking for an excuse to kiss you. And I couldn't bear the thought of your first kiss being with someone else."

I hold my breath for a few beats while I process the confession, my stomach tightening.

I reach up and put my hand on his jaw, brushing my thumb across it. He closes his eyes and leans into my palm. He raises his hand up to mine, wrapping it around my wrist, and then moves both our hands to rest over his heart. Every particle I'm made of combusts. He places his other hand on my waist and takes a step closer.

"We said we weren't going to talk about that kiss ever again," I say, draping my free hand over his shoulder.

He leans his forehead against mine. "I regret agreeing to that."

"You do?"

"I wanted to take it back immediately, but you made me pinky promise. I told you I'd never break a promise to you. And we were both worried about Clay."

"And now we..." I'm afraid to finish the sentence.

"And now we live up to our own motto and take a chance. Being back home in Wedgefield with you this Christmas has made me realize a lot, and it started the second I walked through Mrs. James's door." He takes a deep breath.

"And what did you realize?" I hope my voice sounds steady, but I can't be sure because it almost hurts to speak.

"I never learned how to not love you, Felicity James. I just always have."

I suck in a breath as he tightens his grip on my waist and closes the final bit of space between us. Our chests press together, hearts finally decoded and beating at record speeds, each trying to keep up with the other. I didn't know how much I needed him to say it.

"It's only ever been you, Giancarlo," I tell him. I'm not expecting the freedom that comes with those words. The way my heart transforms from solid to liquid in milliseconds. The way the wilderness inside me blooms like a season changing.

He looks into my eyes, and then at my lips, tipping his head down until our lips are just inches apart. Until finally, finally his lips meet mine. He takes his time, all the while brushing his thumb across my hand that he's still holding over his heart. I move my other hand from his shoulder to the back of his neck, running my fingers up and down. He lets go of my hand to wrap both his arms around me, and I bring my arm up and around his neck. He holds me even tighter as he deepens the kiss, and it's like all these years apart makes us afraid to let go, to not be holding onto each other.

We finally pull ourselves apart, chests heaving, neither one of us letting go.

Everything in the sleeper car is golden, even the flimsy lighting. Giancarlo smiles, and it shimmers under the glow of everything, highlighting the twinkle in his eyes. He pushes my curls back. "Can't tell you how long I've wanted to do that."

"Me too." After all this time, I can't believe it's real.

"We should probably get some sleep. No telling what Nancy Drew will be up against once we get to Lake Margaret."

I laugh. We finally let go of each other, and both our eyes land on the chairs that are supposed to convert to the bed—which I now remember is the only bed in the car.

Giancarlo clears his throat. "You, um, still want to share? It's kinda small for two people." His eyes dart to me, then back at the seats.

I give him a quick kiss on the cheek. "You think now that I can kiss you whenever I want that I'm going to *not* want to sleep next to you?"

He grins. "As always, your wish is forever my command." He pulls the lever on the first chair and works on transforming it. I pull all the shades down, then dig through my bag for my phone to text Clay that we're on the train safely.

Once the seats look like a bed, Giancarlo asks, "Last chance to change your mind."

I shake my head. "Never." It comes out as a whisper, even though I don't intend it to.

He takes off his sneakers and climbs in first so his body is parallel with the window. The space really is smaller than I thought. He looks at me, the two of us nervous about how charged the air in this sleeper car really is. I sit on the edge of the bed and take off my shoes, then lie down with my back to him. It's impossible for us to not touch.

I glance back at him over my shoulder. "Am I taking up too much space?"

"I'll say what you just said to me: never."

I laugh, although it comes out kind of strained.

"Besides, we're a little past that, anyway. You're already all over my heart."

I let out a sigh.

"That's a good sigh, right?" he asks.

"Very good."

We're quiet for a few minutes before he says, "I really want to hold you."

"And I really want to be held," I say.

He inches closer to me, and when I feel his toned arm wrap around me, my heart steps on the gas again. I place my hand over his, drawing it close to my heart.

"I can feel your heart beating fast," he says, nuzzling his face in the back of my neck.

I shiver. "Only for you."

"That makes two of us."

The last thing I think before I drift to sleep is how this is what I've been missing.

GIANCARLO

Felicity is stretching in my arms when I wake up. For a second, I'm disoriented, and then I remember how she got there. I smile.

"Can I please have more waking up next to you in my life?" I say.

She turns around and kisses my neck.

"More of that too."

She taps my chest lightly, and I laugh.

"Come on, the train's going to stop soon." She starts to get up, but I tighten my hold on her.

"Do we have to leave?"

"Yeah. We're on a mission, remember?"

I groan. "So you're saying we can't just change the mission, move into this room, and travel the world for the rest of our lives?"

"That's exactly what I'm saying." She laughs again, and I always want to hear that symphony. I'll do whatever she wants as long as the melody of her laugh is a guarantee.

She wriggles out of my arms and stands up. "We gotta get moving."

We both clean up, and by the time we each take our turns in the restroom, the conductor is over the speaker, telling us we've arrived in Lake Margaret. The train comes to a stop, and we grab our backpacks. I slide the door to our sleeper car open.

"This is it," she says, glancing up at me.

I reach for her hand, and together we leave the station. Above the door on the way out is a sign with a Christmas wreath below it that says: Welcome to Lake Margaret. It's a quaint town, very much like Wedgefield, Cardwick, and even Marvelwest. Outside of the station, we find ourselves in that dewy blue moment of morning, right before the sun is about to come up, and the darkness of the night is on its way out. There are a handful of people walking about.

I point to a diner up ahead. "Want to grab breakfast and figure out where we're headed?" I ask.

"Good idea," she says. I lead us to the cottage-like building.

A gust of warm air and cinnamon hits me when I open the mint-green door.

It's not busy at all, and the song *Silver Bells* rings through the speakers. A woman in a yellow uniform greets us with a big smile from behind the counter.

"Good morning and welcome!" she says. "You two looking to dine at the tables or the counter?" she asks.

"The counter," Felicity says. She turns to me. "We don't have much time before we have to get back on the next train."

I nod.

Donna is written on the woman's silver nametag, which also contains several Christmas stickers and a tiny Christmas tree hanging from the edge.

"What can I get you two lovebirds?" Donna asks.

Felicity and I blush at each other, then say in unison, "Pancakes."

"Buttermilk, blueberry, chocolate chip?"

"Buttermilk," Felicity answers for both of us.

"And two cups of coffee," I say.

"Comin' right up." Donna grabs the menus that were pre-set at our spots and takes off to the kitchen.

Felicity pulls out her phone from her coat pocket. "Okay, so I think the first thing we need to do is find where The One Ornament Gift Shop is and how far we are from it."

"Did I hear you say you're lookin' for The One Ornament Gift Shop?" Donna is standing in front of us with two white coffee mugs and a full pot of fresh coffee.

"Yeah. You know it?" Felicity says.

"'Course I do, honey, it's a small town." She sets the cups down and pours coffee into our mugs. "It's just down the way. You're already on Main. Should take you about ten minutes."

"Thank you so much," Felicity says. "You know anything about the owner?" She picks up her cup and holds it with both hands.

"Sure do," Donna says. She reaches into her apron for her notepad, flipping the pages to read something.

"That's great," I say.

"Don't get too excited now."

"If you're looking for Enzo, he keeps to himself. Spends most of his time in the back of the store, making ornaments. Usually, Roger is the one that handles the day-to-day of the store, including the customers," she says.

I scrunch my face. "Does Enzo ever talk to anyone?" I ask.

Donna shrugs. "Sometimes."

"Order up," the chef says, which gets Donna's attention. She turns around to see two plates waiting in the cutout window to the kitchen, and she's off before Felicity and I can grill her any further.

Felicity sips her coffee and stares off into the distance. It's one of the things I love about her—the way there's this sight line that appears between her brows when her mind is at work.

"What are you thinking?" I ask.

"That we only have twelve hours before we have to head back home, and we just found out Enzo is a recluse."

"Let's not worry about that right now. Remember our theme song?"

She smiles. "Take a chance."

"Exactly."

Donna comes back and sets down two plates with pancake stacks. "Enjoy," she says before dashing off to greet the customers who just entered.

"Looks like we got here just in time." I look around at how some of the tables have filled up.

"We should probably hurry." Felicity pours an ungodly amount of maple syrup over her pancakes.

I snicker and push my fork into my own stack.

"And just what's so funny?" she asks, my eyes landing on the tiny drop of maple syrup at the corner of her mouth.

I shrug. "I'm just happy to see that some things never change."

"What?" she asks, a smile playing at her lips.

"I see you're still drowning your pancakes in maple syrup."

She falls into a fit of laughter and holds up her fork, which has a piece of pancake on it. "Rest in peace, pancakes."

I laugh because it's classic Felicity. She wipes the corner of her eye. When the two of us stop laughing, she's still got maple syrup on her lips. I don't even bother telling her it's there. I reach out and brush it away with my thumb, then kiss the spot where it was.

"Delicious," I say.

We stare back at each other, and all I want is for us to be back on that train again so I can have more private moments to kiss her.

Her smile fades a little. "I saw you drawing last night before we left," she says.

I take a bite of my pancakes and nod. "Yeah."

"Did you, uh, make any progress?" she asks.

"Yeah, yeah. I made some good progress."

"That's good," she says, setting her fork down.

I pause. "You hear back from your boss on your ornament pitch?"

"Not yet." She tucks a few loose curls behind her ear. "I'm sure she'll be in touch any day now."

In the backs of our minds, we're both thinking the

same thing. We're living in the bubble of last night for now. And it's easy to do that because no one is around. We can be whoever we want in this town, even if it's just for twelve hours. But things aren't exactly simple. I still have a mural to finish, not to mention the rest of gigs I had lined up. She has a career and a life to get back to in Ivanhoe Springs. And what on earth are we going to tell Clay? In my mind, I'd decided I couldn't spend another second not letting her know how I felt, but I realize now that I didn't really think about if she'd decided that too. We want each other, but how will it all work? I can't just ask her to drop everything because I all of a sudden got the guts to tell her how I've felt all along.

Donna comes back then. "Can I get you two anything else?"

"We're good," I say.

She rips a piece of paper off from her notepad and sets it down on the table. Felicity reaches for her backpack, but I stop her. "Let me," I say, already removing my card from my wallet and dropping it on the bill Donna just set down.

"Be right back," Donna says.

"Thank you," Felicity says.

When we were younger and found ourselves out together, she'd always insist on paying the bill. I never let her, of course. Looking back at it now, I think it was her way of keeping us compartmentalized in her mind.

I lean in close to her ear and whisper, "I know you can take care of yourself, but I like doing things for you. I'll do whatever you want if you let me."

Her eyes spark, and then she tugs the collar of my coat, pulling me close to her until her lips are on mine. It's a soft kiss, definitely not like the one we shared last night, but I welcome it, arms wide open and all the same. We pull away when Donna clears her throat.

She's smiling, her eyes peeking above her teal wire-framed glasses. "Don't stop on account of me." She chuckles as she hands me back my card and a receipt for me to keep.

I'm usually not into PDA, but I can't keep my hands off Felicity. We find ourselves blushing again.

"You two should check out the Christmas tree lights display at the tree farm. It's something to see this time of year. And stop by again before you get on that train. I'll make sure to tell the next waitress on shift to send you off with something warm. Good luck, lovebirds." She turns around, grabs a pot of coffee from the warmer, and makes her way to the tables to refill cups.

Felicity hops off her stool. "We should get going. No telling how much groveling we'll have to do on Grams's behalf."

"Sounds like it's going to be extra." I stand up,

catching Felicity's hand. "Hey. We have twelve hours. We'll think of all the other stuff later, okay?"

"I like that plan," she says.

And the two of us are off to find what sounds like the grump of the town.

FELICITY

Donna was right. It only takes us about ten minutes before Giancarlo and I are standing in front of The One Ornament. It stands out from the rest of the shops along the street with its log cabin style storefront. It's probably about twenty degrees out, but my hands start sweating in my gloves. I let out a deep breath. *Take a chance for Grams.*

Giancarlo squeezes my hand. "Should we go in?"

I nod.

Inside, it's like home. It's tiny, but cozy. Ornaments fill the wood-paneled walls around the whole store and hang from the light fixtures on the ceiling. There's also an electric fireplace on the far right of the store, complete with a Christmas tree next to it. Upon closer inspection, the ornaments are glass blown. I pick one up, raising it so I can study the swirl of red, green, and glitter.

"It has to be him," I whisper.

"That one's beautiful, isn't it?" a husky voice says.

When I look up, a stocky man with a thick salt-and-pepper mustache stands before me. He offers me a warm St. Nicholas smile. He's wearing a plaid button-down shirt, red suspenders, and jeans. It's all pretty basic and yet somehow still dapper.

"It is. Do you know the artist?" I ask.

"You're looking at him." He pulls on his suspenders and puffs his chest out.

"You're very talented." I scan his features, analyzing him, and I only realize I'm doing it when Giancarlo clears his throat.

"Nice shop you have here," Giancarlo says.

"Well, thank you." The man turns his attention back to me. I almost don't catch it, but the corners of his eyes twitch like he's trying to fight the urge to narrow them. "You look really familiar. You're not one of those Hollywood types, are you?"

I laugh. "No, no. We're actually just passing through. I'm an ornament maker as well. I work for Muralo out of the Ivanhoe Springs branch."

His smile widens. "Ah, so you're a fellow glassblower. Muralo is a great company."

"Yeah," I say, remembering the countless times my boss has shot down my ideas. "My grandmother taught me," I say.

One corner of his mouth turns up, but it's slight. He sticks his hands in his pockets. "That's nice. So, anything in particular bring you to Lake Margaret, or you two just on holiday?"

"We're actually looking for someone," Giancarlo says.

"That so?" His smile falters.

This whole trip has felt like a suspended breath. I remind myself to breathe. "We're looking for Enzo Bianchi, the owner of this store."

No trace of a smile now. "Well, that's also me. But what can I do for you?"

I swallow. Giancarlo squeezes my shoulder. "I'm Felicity James." I keep my eyes on his. "And Hazel James, also known as Hazel Woods, is my grandmother."

His face darkens then. "What did you just say?"

Giancarlo answers for me. "This is Hazel's granddaughter. And judging by the look on your face, I think you know who we mean."

He straightens, his now bewildered eyes staring back at me. I was half hoping his warm smile would return. Wishful thinking.

"I think it might be time for the two of you to leave. You're just passing through, right?"

I glance at Giancarlo, and he nods for me to go on, to plead my case. I'm not sure it's going to do any good, but I promised myself I'd try anyway.

"We traveled a long way to come here, Mr. Bianchi. Hear us out," I say.

"She still in Wedgefield?" he asks.

I sigh. "Yes. I found something in her attic—something she intended for you. But she never gave it to you. When I asked her about it, I could tell that the memory was painful for her. She loved you. Maybe you two could—"

"The two of us cannot *do* anything. It was pretty clear your grandmother wanted nothing to do with me." His jaw locks.

"If you don't mind me asking, sir, how do you know? According to Grams, you disappeared."

"I didn't disappear. I told her where I was going," he says.

Again, I look to Giancarlo, but his knitted brows say he's just as puzzled as I am. "Grams didn't mention you all chatting before she left."

"It wasn't a conversation." He walks over to the register, and we follow. He flops down on a stool near the register and takes out a handkerchief to wipe his face. "My father got really sick. Heart failure. My family left Wedgefield because my mother had heard of a cardiologist here in Lake Margaret who might be able to help. So, she got it in her head that we needed to move so he could treat my father. Once my mother got something in her head, well, let's just say it was hard to get it out."

"And you told Grams this?" I ask.

Enzo's eyebrows arch in anguish. "Yeah. I called her house a couple of times and left messages for her to call me back. It wasn't exactly something you said over the phone. I even went to her house the day we left." He closes his eyes for a second. "I banged on that door forever. Eventually, I had to accept no one was home, so I stuck a note in the door telling her everything."

That lights up my brain. "Grams never said anything about a note from you."

"But you said yourself she clammed up about the whole thing," Giancarlo says.

I shake my head. "True, but I'm willing to put money on the fact that Grams never got that note."

Enzo pauses to think for a moment. He folds his arms across his chest and rubs his chin. "I mean, I guess that's possible. I always assumed she got it. I even called her house one more time after that, but she never returned the call. I thought she didn't want to hear from me. My mother had also convinced me it was best. My family needed me, and it was tough to make long distance work, especially in those days."

My heart expands in my chest, billowing with hope. "There's a chance she might have been hiding it from me. But my gut tells me she never got that note."

Enzo's quiet for a bit before he finally says, "Still, none of that matters. It's water under the bridge. Look at you." He motions to me. "You're proof she's got her own life now. She's moved on. I've moved on. There's no point in digging all this up."

"That's what she said too. But I think she'd change her mind if she knew what you just told me." I pause, then flip through my phone for the photo I snapped of the letter Grams never delivered. "And maybe you'd change your mind if you knew how much she cared for you back then." I offer my phone to him.

His lips stretch to a flat line of annoyance before he takes it from me. As he reads, each of the hard lines on his face softens. He swallows, his eyes turning glassy. "Your grandmother know you're here?"

"She doesn't," I admit.

He pushes the phone back into my hands. "That's my point."

"I had to make sure it was you, Mr. Bianchi. Please—"

"Look, I know you mean well, but too much time has

passed. If it was meant to be, it would be. I do appreciate you taking your holiday time to come here and find me, but I've been just fine on my own." The bell on the front door jingles. "And I've got other customers now, so I must be getting back to work. Have a safe trip back home."

He turns his back and is off to greet the people who just walked in while I stand there, not wanting to believe everything just fell apart.

"We should go," Giancarlo says.

I nod, but my gaze falls on a stack of sticky notes on the counter. I look at Giancarlo, who narrows his eyes.

"What are you thinking, Felicity James?"

I grab the sticky notepad and the pen next to it and write: *Take a chance*. Then I unzip my backpack and pull out the ornament Grams made all those years ago and leave it next to the note. If this last-ditch effort fails, I'll have to deal with Grams's wrath, but that's a problem for future Felicity. One more note, one more chance.

GIANCARLO

We're standing outside of The One Ornament, Felicity pressed to my chest, me tracing circles on her back. I am in and out of emotions. There's the me that's finally able to hold this woman on a public street. That me is realizing how much he likes it. How much he likes thinking about where this could go. This me is falling, falling, falling. Every minute spent with her, my heart drops another notch. And then there's the me who wants to fix this for her, but forcing Enzo to talk to Mrs. James is not exactly a viable option. This me feels guilty for thinking about how happy I am right now when she's not.

I check the time on my phone. We have a while before we have to get back on the train and head home. I might not have all the answers, but I have one.

I ease back so I can look her in the eyes, but I keep an arm wrapped around her shoulder. "I know you're disappointed. But maybe he's just not ready. It's his and your grandmother's story. Remember when you asked me what I remember about my mom?"

"Yeah..."

"Well, there was one other thing I remember her saying. She told me people don't play the roles that you want them to play in your movie of life. Back then, I didn't know what she meant, but as I got older, I understood. None of it's personal. You just happen to be the one there in the moment. Could have been anyone."

"Pretty sure he just kicked us out of his store. Feels pretty personal to me."

"You have to remember he was hurt. And we did come out of nowhere with this new information. People need time to process." I kiss the top of her head.

She's quiet for a bit, then says, "Fine. You have a point."

"You know what we need?"

"A Santa that grants Christmas wishes? A miracle on 34th Street?"

I smirk. "I was going to say a little Christmas, but yes, those things couldn't hurt."

"What do you propose?" she asks, fighting a smile.

That's more like it.

"Donna said the Christmas tree lot had a tree display. What if we grab some hot chocolate and hang out there until it's time to head home?"

She raises an eyebrow. "That depends."

"On?"

"On whether or not I can have another kiss."

I step in front of her so we're both facing each other, and I wrap my arms around her waist. She rests both her hands flat on my chest. "That's one thing you never have to ask for."

She shifts her gaze to my chest. "If I don't have to ask, does that mean we're making this a thing?"

"I thought it already was."

Her eyes connect with mine again, curls in a rhapsody with the wind.

"I'm yours, even if you stop wanting me."

"Never," she says.

"Okay, so someone is going to have to let Andrew down," I tease.

Her mouth hangs open, a playful smile on her lips. "He's a nice guy, you know. He's just not you."

"This is the second-best Christmas I've ever had."

"Second-best?"

"Yup, best Christmas was the first time we kissed.

Haven't been able to match it since—until now."

I lean down, and she brushes her thumb over my cheekbone. I close my eyes to savor the moment before I cover her lips with mine. Heat unfurls within me, activating every single atom I'm made of. When I'm kissing her, nothing even matters. There's only her and the moment I never want to leave.

I have absolutely no interest in Christmas trees right now. What fills me up most is Felicity leading me by the hand through a variety of bright lights. I don't see any of them. They all blur together in one big cluster of colors. I'm thinking about the way her palm feels against my palm, like it was specifically made for it. The way her curls are all wild from us being out in the cold air. The way she licks her lips after taking a sip of her hot chocolate. And especially about the way my heart is on an endless loop of Felicity now that I've given it permission. It hums her name with every beat.

We've already been out here for forty minutes. Since it was too cold to spend hours out here, we decided to warm up indoors first with lunch, a couple Christmas movies that the local theater had running for the holidays, and a trip to the bookstore. We have one more stop after this, which is to grab dinner at the diner.

Felicity stops in front of a tree, leaning in and examining one of the ornaments.

"The whole tree is full of glass-blown ornaments. I bet they're Enzo's. No one else around here is making ornaments like these." She sighs. "He's so talented."

"So are you," I say.

She turns back to look at me.

"I mean it. Look at how your ornaments have made others feel. The gifts you've made, the ones you donated to the Wedgefield Center. They're special, just like you. Maybe it's time to live up to our theme song—take a chance on yourself."

"I'm a creative, not a businesswoman," she says, tracing her finger on one of the ornaments.

"You can get help from Clay. I'm sure he'd be willing to help."

She lets out a deep breath. "Speaking of Clay..."

"I thought we agreed to think of the other stuff later?"

"We did, but we're going home soon. We should probably decide if we're going to be up front about this thing or wait a bit," she says.

I don't say anything at first. I'd been intentionally not allowing my mind to think about what Clay might say. He's been my best friend for forever, even when Felicity and I weren't really talking. But then I remember how it felt kissing Felicity on that sidewalk and not worrying or caring who saw. The whole point of deciding to come clean about how I feel was because I got tired of digging holes in myself for this secret. All that aside, we're not kids anymore.

"We should just tell him—as soon as we get back," I say.

Felicity smiles. "My brother ultimately wants to see us happy. He'll come around."

Something about the way she says that makes me think she's trying to convince herself too. My phone dings.

I wince when Riley's name appears on the screen. I ignored that email from her before we got on the train and was so wrapped up I forgot to text her back.

> **Riley:** *Giancarlo, I think you should get back here. The mayor thinks you've had enough time to regroup. He's threatening to pull the plug.*

I lock my jaw, my mouth suddenly dry.

Felicity's smile vanishes when she sees my face. "What is it?" she asks.

"I have to get back to Marvelwest. The mayor is threatening to end the project."

"Before Christmas? I thought you got him to change it to a New Year's mural?"

"I did. But when I accept these jobs, they usually include accommodations. I think me not being there working is making him a little too uncomfortable."

"So that means you'll have to get on another night train." She stares off into the distance.

"Yeah. The first one I can find a seat on once we get back."

"Okay." Her voice sounds far away.

Two disappointments in one day, and I can't do anything about it.

"Hey," I say, lifting her chin with the side of my index finger. "We'll have more Christmases, right?"

She gives me a half smile. "Maybe a lot of them."

"As many as you'll let me have." I lean in for a kiss. As my lips connect with hers, all I can think is how it will never get old. I force myself to pull away and say, "Come on, we have a train to catch."

FELICITY

When we get back to Gram's house, it's late and everything is serene. My fingers are laced with Giancarlo's as we walk up the path to the front door. I stop on the front steps and look up at the shimmering sky. The stars always seemed brighter in Wedgefield than anywhere else, and I'm reminded again of how many hours Giancarlo and I spent staring up at them. He stops and looks up too. I want to stay here a little longer—where the two of us are caught in a medley of memories under this luminous sky. I catch his eye, and he reads my mind. His lips find mine and as I'm about to pull him close, the front door flings open.

"What in the world?" Clay's wearing red flannel pajamas and holding a Santa Claus mug.

His voice startles us apart.

"Clay," I say. But I can't find the words. The plan was to tell him immediately, but I'm also caught off guard.

He turns around, and we follow him inside to the living room. He reaches into his pocket, takes out a twenty-dollar bill and slides it onto the side table where Grams is seated in comfy nightwear, complete with velvet slippers. She's holding a cup with both hands near her mouth, which breaks into a slick smile. I look at Giancarlo, and he shrugs.

Clay laughs. "Grams called it. I thought the two of you would drag it out until at least Christmas."

"Wait." I loosen my scarf and take off my coat. "What?"

Grams sips her cup. "We bet on when the two of you would finally cut the bull and get together."

Giancarlo and I let out an audible breath at the same time, relaxing as Grams and Clay continue their fit of laughter.

"It's not *that* funny. You two knew?" I ask, my cheeks warming.

"Come on, sis. The way the two of you have been pining over each other since the second we walked through the door? We have eyes. Matter of fact, I had eyes when we were younger too. Nothing has changed."

Giancarlo shakes his head, now shedding his layers of winter clothes too. "Why didn't you say anything?"

"It wasn't my business. I honestly thought y'all would work it out. But then we all kind of went our separate ways after college, and I noticed you lost touch. I just assumed it wasn't meant to be. But we came back here, and it was *very* clear y'all kept that same energy. I gotta admit, I wasn't sure it would happen."

I roll my eyes. "You could have saved us a lot of time."

"Correction: *you* could have saved you a lot of time. Now, what lesson did we learn today, kids?" He smirks.

"So how was Marvelwest?" Grams asks.

Once more, I look to Giancarlo. He nods for me to continue.

"Grams, I have to tell you something." There's a tiny twinge in my stomach.

Her attention is on me as she takes another sip, smile wide. She looks beautiful in her lace nightgown and matching robe under all the lights radiating from the tree. It's definitely Enzo's loss. "Something wrong?" she asks, no doubt noting the way my smile slips.

"We weren't in Marvelwest."

"Where were you? You know, that's really not safe. What if something happened and I didn't know where you were?"

"We were in Lake Margaret," I blurt out, stopping

her lecture.

"What's in Lake Margaret?"

I swallow and tug at my sweater collar. "Okay, before you get upset..."

Those are trigger words for her because now something switches in her eyes, and she's up out of her chair. "What did you do, Felicity?"

I swallow, and it hurts. The words stuck in my throat are already leaving a bruise. "We found Enzo."

The cup slips from her hand, crashing to the floor and spilling tea all over her plush rug. Clay grabs the napkins she has on the coffee table, sopping up the mess.

A storm rolls through her eyes. And then it's all over her face. Rain and lightning and thunder. "I specifically told you not to get involved." She points a finger at me, her other hand at her side, balled in a fist. Thunder. "Let me guess, he wasn't interested in what you had to say?"

I shake my head. I can't even speak. I've never seen her so upset.

Water springs in her eyes. Rain.

"Grams, I'm sorry. I thought I was helping." I step forward and try to hug her, but she pushes me away.

"I don't know if I can ever forgive you for this, Felicity." Lightning.

She stalks off up the stairs, leaving us all in shreds—the aftermath of her storm.

It's not exactly how I thought this Christmas would go. When I agreed to spend it in Wedgefield with Grams, I thought we'd be spending it baking all my Trinidadian favorites. I pictured the air in the house full of the sweet scent of cinnamon, raisins, and rum-soaked fruits from sweet bread and black cake. I pictured us sitting in the living room for hours, catching up and looking at old family photos. I pictured opening presents on Christmas morning, then watching heartwarming Christmas movies for the rest of the day. Instead, she's been locked in her room, only coming downstairs for food. She's not speaking to anyone, and if I'm honest, I don't blame her. I've turned her Christmas into a disaster zone.

The last words she said to me are on repeat in my mind: *I don't know if I can ever forgive you for this.* If that's true, I don't know if I'll ever forgive myself.

I'm sitting on the porch in the freezing cold, a blanket wrapped around me. On my phone is a little bubble with a one above the envelope icon. It's the email I've been waiting for after submitting my recent ornament ideas. I click it immediately, my stomach clenching. It only drags my mood down further, if that's even possible.

Felicity,

Let's chat in the new year. I've always said I admire your innovation, but we're not looking to completely change the way we make ornaments. I'm afraid these still aren't quite the direction I was hoping to go. We can put our heads together when you get back. Happy holidays!

Jill Stevenson, President
Muralo, Inc.

A text from Giancarlo flashes across the top of my screen.

Giancarlo: *I miss you.*

He's texted me this every day since leaving a few days ago, and it's the one thing I have to look forward to since I've ruined everything else. But then our theme song pops into my head: Take a chance.

I type out an email to my boss:

Dear Jill,

I hope you are enjoying your holiday, and thank you for the feedback. Unfortunately, I don't think

Muralo is the right space for me anymore. I really appreciate you taking a chance on me, but I think it's time I take a chance on me. Please consider this my formal resignation.

-Felicity

"Hey," Clay says, peeking his head out from Grams's hunter-green front door.

"Hey," I say.

"You doing okay?" he asks.

"I just quit my job."

He blinks. "I'm sorry, you what?"

"I quit," I repeat. The more I say it, the more it feels good, never mind the parallel feeling of fear.

"So what will you do?"

I shrug. "Don't know."

"I know I joke around a lot, but I want to tell you how proud of you I am. You've come a long way from that nerdy girl with braces."

He lets out a belly laugh, and I roll my eyes.

"In all seriousness, I'm glad you're taking more chances." He smiles and steps out onto the porch to give me a hug.

I return it and squeeze him hard. In a few days, he'll be headed back to his company and his life in New York.

"Thanks, Clay."

"I actually came out here to get you to come talk to Grams. She's not talking to me either, and I think we need to squash this."

I stand up. "You know I want to."

"Come on, she's in the kitchen." He grabs the back of my shoulders and guides me forward.

Grams is at the sink, unloading the dishwasher. She's washed all her special Christmas dishes in preparation for Christmas dinner. It's a good sign, even if her plan is to sit across from us at the dinner table in silence.

"Hi, Grams," I say, my voice hushed, cautious.

She glances over her shoulder. "Hello."

I glance at Clay. That's a lot better than her treating me like Casper the Friendly Ghost, no matter the amount of frost on that hello.

Clay clears his throat. "Grams, I know you're mad, but we promise we had your best interest at heart. We just wanted to see you happy."

She turns around in slow motion to face us, leaning her hip against the counter. "I just wish you two would have listened. Do you want to know why I didn't want to dig all this up?"

"Actually, now we have a pretty good idea why." I take a seat in the breakfast nook, Clay following suit.

"I was so hopelessly in love with him. I just wanted

him to know it. We'd been seeing each other casually and calling it 'hanging out.' As the two of you can relate to, I had Trinidadian parents. So you know they're all about us getting a good education before thinking about dating, which meant we were hesitant to label anything. But I felt like I would burst if I didn't tell him how I felt."

I nod. Relatable. I wanted Giancarlo so much sometimes it hurt.

"I was going to give him the note, then the ornament and the confession when we met. I spent hours trying to perfect that thing." She chuckles, her vision dipping into that alternate timeline. And I dressed up and showed up to his family's bakery with the note I was gonna leave there for him. When I walked in, his mother was there to help with customers. She told me that his dad was sick, and even though I was a *nice* girl, I needed to let Enzo be. He was going to have to step up and help the family, and I was just a distraction."

She swipes a tear with her index finger.

"She said it was time for him to focus on his family. So I left that day, pretty broken, and I never heard from him again. To me, it meant that he felt the same. He needed to be there for his family, and I was in the way."

I get up and wrap an arm around her shoulders. Clay hugs her from the other side.

"Oh, Grams. I had no idea."

"Some things should stay history. I've made my peace with it. And I'll never be sorry about moving on with my life. I have an amazing family that drives me nuts." She laughs. "But I know they care."

"Grams, if you could see the way Enzo got all sad when we told him who we were. I doubt he knew his mother said those things to you, and I don't think you'd believe this story anymore. Plus, he said he left a letter in your door the day he left."

Her eyes ping-pong between Clay and me like she's lost in a memory maze. "He did?" she whispers.

I nod.

"It doesn't have to be the way the story ends," Clay says.

But she shakes her head. "Some stories don't have happy endings." She reaches for both of our hands and holds onto us tightly. "There is something the two of you can do for me, though."

Clay and I look at each other, then at her.

"What's that?" I say.

"You can both learn from me. Clay, I want you to keep moving forward with your athletic company and stop being so afraid to love. Don't give up. And Felicity, I want you to be bold. I want you to find your independence from Muralo, and I want you and Giancarlo to hold onto that precious love you've found."

"About that," I say, my smile growing. "I just quit."

Grams claps. "Now it's a merry Christmas!"

The three of us laugh, but my smile fades when I remember Giancarlo isn't here.

Clay pats my shoulder. "I bet he wishes he were here too."

I nod.

"That's why I have an early Christmas present for you." He disappears out of the kitchen and comes back with a slender, glittery red box. It sparkles under Grams's chandelier as he hands it over to me. I tilt my head to the side, studying him as I take the box. When I open it, a train ticket slips out.

I place my hand over my heart. "What's this?"

"You two have stayed apart long enough. Sometimes, you have to take matters into your own hands. Go get em'."

I pull him into a fierce hug. "I can't thank you enough," I whisper.

He laughs. "Okay, okay, enough mushiness. You have a train to catch…again."

GIANCARLO

Turns out, I just needed a little inspiration. This whole time, I'd been trying to come up with the right image when I didn't really need an image at all. The answer was me. I spent years perfecting my lettering, and yet, it has never been the focal point of my art. It was Felicity who inspired the idea as we kept reminding each other to take a chance. It was the perfect quote for a New Year's mural. I stand back and admire my creation in the lobby of the mayor's office. Seeing *Take a Chance* in my own handwriting scrawled across a public official's wall reminds me that I can do anything. I hope it reminds everyone who will see this mural in the new year.

With the exception of a few hours of sleep, I've spent the last few days working to finish it. The paint on my hands will require a lot of scrubbing. I check the time on my phone. Riley and Mayor Ortiz will be showing up any second now. There's also a message from Felicity in response to my text from earlier:

Felicity: *I miss you more.*

My heart thumps faster in my chest—something it's been doing a lot of lately. I start cleaning up the space while I wait, washing out paint rollers and brushes, emptying the paint trays, rolling up tarps. I'm taking a gulp from my water bottle when the door chimes, and the mayor and Riley walk in, the click of Riley's heels against the marble tile echoing. They don't even see me standing there in the middle of the lobby. Their attention goes straight to my mural.

At first, they're quiet. Oh God, they hate it. I open my mouth to explain, but the mayor turns to me, a smile stretching straight to the corners of his dark eyes.

"This is quite outstanding," he says. He pushes his hands into the pockets of his pinstriped suit. "It's the perfect quote to start the new year."

Riley pats my shoulder. "I admit you had us worried for a second there, but you pulled it off," she says.

I knit my brows together. "Thanks? I think?"

The mayor chuckles. "Don't worry, it's a compliment." He takes a step forward for closer inspection.

"Remember, the paint is still wet," I say.

He nods.

"I still have minor details to add in some of the coloration and blending. But I have some place to be for Christmas, so if it's okay with you, I'd like to add those details on January 2nd. That will give you a few days before the reveal when the office opens for the new year."

"I think that can be arranged." He keeps studying the artwork—*my* artwork. "Every year, we do a new one for the holidays. You know, to showcase different artists. But I like this so much I think I want to keep it permanently."

"Really?" I'm still trying to process how I went from completely blocked and not knowing how to pull this off, to the mayor liking it so much he wants to make it permanent.

"Really. Let's talk when you get back in the new year. I also have some other projects that might interest you, and I'd love to recommend you to some colleagues. Riley, will you make a note for us to set up a meeting come January?"

Riley starts tapping on her phone screen. "Yes, sir," she says, adjusting her yellow blazer.

He extends his hand, and I shake it.

"Oh, one more thing. What inspired this quote?"

I rub the back of my neck. "My girlfriend, actually. We kind of call it our theme song." It's not lost on me that it's the first time I call her my girlfriend out loud. I want to say it over and over and over again.

Riley smiles.

"Sounds like a good song," Mayor Ortiz says.

I run a hand through my hair and nod. "It's my favorite."

I bought the train ticket back to Wedgefield while I was on the train to Marvelwest. I didn't want to get Felicity's hopes up in case things didn't go as planned. Thank goodness for Christmas magic, because it's why I'm on the train now headed her way. The only downside is that I have to stop at the station in Cardwick to change trains, but at least I'm going to get to her by Christmas. It's only about a four-hour train ride in total, but it feels like four years.

When the train is almost to the Cardwick Train Station, I text her:

> **Giancarlo:** *Miss you… what are you up to?*

Felicity: *Miss you more. I'm reading. Made up with Grams btw.*

Giancarlo: *I knew she'd come around.*

Felicity: *I didn't.* 😮

Giancarlo: *She's tough, but she loves you too much to stay mad.*

Felicity: *What are you up to?*

Giancarlo: *Texting you*

Felicity: *Haha very funny.*

Giancarlo: *LOL*

Felicity: *I wish you were here*

Giancarlo: *I wish that too. I'll make it up to you.*

Felicity: *How?*

Giancarlo: *It involves lots of hugs…*

Felicity: *And?*

Giancarlo: *Plenty of kissing*

> **Felicity:** *I like the sound of that.*

> **Giancarlo:** *And a surprise I think you're gonna like* ☺

> **Felicity:** *What surprise????*

> **Giancarlo:** *You'll see* ☺

The train starts to slow as it pulls into Cardwick Station. Just one more short ride and I'll be home. Once I'm in the waiting area, I grab a snack, and as I'm looking up, I spot her—the brown curls I love wrapping around my fingers. The perfect brown skin that underneath contains a universe I wouldn't mind exploring for the rest of my life. My muse. My everything. It's then, while I'm wading in disbelief and awe, that her eyes land on me. Several groups of people between us, and still our eyes find each other's. She squints, then her mouth hangs open, and at last she smiles.

We race to each other, zigzagging through the crowd of people until we're close enough for me to wrap my arms around her, lift her off the floor, and spin her in the middle of a busy train station on Christmas Eve. We waste no time. Our lips crash into each other. She buries her head in my neck, leaving a trail of kisses. When we finally slow down, she looks into my eyes.

"What are you doing here?"

"I needed you. What are you doing here?"

"I needed you."

We laugh.

"I worked day and night to finish that mural so I could get back to you," I tell her.

"Clay bought me a ticket to make it to you by Christmas."

"Remind me to thank him later."

"Doubt he'll let you forget it."

"True." I laugh again. "Think they'll let you change the ticket?"

"I hope so. It's Christmas."

I kiss her cheek. "Felicity?"

"Yes?" she whispers.

"I'm really glad I took a chance and came home this Christmas."

"Me too. And I'm glad you made me take a chance on myself."

"I love you," I say.

"I love you too." She threads her fingers with mine. "Let's go home."

FELICITY

Trinidadian Christmas music roaring from Grams's Bluetooth speakers. Macaroni pie in the oven. On our dinner table: callaloo, red beans, sweet potatoes, and stew chicken. Clay, Grams, Giancarlo, and I are in the living room with crystal glasses that hold ponche de crème. In this draft, I am sitting next to the love of my life, his arm draped over my shoulders, his fingers laced with mine. In this draft, I am made of Christmas lights, and perfect winter skies, and everything good that comes with this season. In this draft, the boy is mine.

"Let's do a toast," Clay says.

The four of us stand, drinks raised.

"I'm so glad we were able to all be here to celebrate with each other," Grams says. "I would have understood, but I would have been so sad to not have you here, Felicity and Giancarlo."

"I guess I'm Mr. Invisible this Christmas." Clay rolls his eyes.

We all burst into laughter.

Grams bumps his shoulder with hers. "You know we love you very much, Clayton. I do wish your parents were here, though."

"They sent their love to everyone," I say. I leave out the string of questions they also sent via texts after I told them about Giancarlo.

"To family!" Grams says.

"To family!" we all repeat.

Everyone takes a sip, but our fun is interrupted by the doorbell.

There's a brief silence before Clay sets his glass down on the coffee table. "Are you expecting anyone, Grams?"

She shakes her head. "At first, Nettie said she might stop by, but she called a bit ago to say she's caught up with her family."

Clay goes to the front door, the rest of us looking at each other, baffled. When he comes back, he's not alone. Under the warm glow of the lights from Grams's Christmas decorations stands Enzo Bianchi. I reach my hand up to Giancarlo's shoulder and squeeze.

I whisper, "He took a chance."

"Looks like you were right." He kisses my forehead. "You always are."

Grams and Enzo haven't moved a muscle. They're staring into each other's eyes, both with water tapdancing on the rims.

I clear my throat. "It's really good to see you, Enzo."

He snaps out of it after hearing his name, nods at me, then looks back to Grams. "I hope it's okay that I came."

Grams is still not moving—I'm not even sure she's breathing.

"I know there's probably a lot to talk about, but after the note Felicity left, I figured I'd just start with her suggestion—taking a chance."

We all wait for Grams to say something because, let's be real, she could shut this all down right now, and we'd have to be okay with it. Right now, she is stone still, until tears start streaming. Enzo takes a few careful steps until there's not much distance between them. He reaches his arm out, taking his time until it finds its way to Grams's cheek. She closes her eyes, gripping his wrist. Enzo pulls her gently, slowly, into an embrace, and all I can think is how many gifts this Christmas has brought.

"Would you like to stay for dinner?" Grams says.

Enzo smiles. "There's nowhere else I'd rather be. He

gazes around the room at each of us. "If you'll have me."

"Of course," I say.

"Felicity, I can't thank you enough for what you did," Enzo says.

"I knew this love story wasn't over," I say.

Grams blushes, and they exchange a quick glance.

Enzo clears his throat. "And we'll take things one step at a time, but I'd love to talk to you more about your ornaments, Felicity. I have a few ideas."

"I'd love that," I say.

"How did you find the house, though, Mr. Bianchi?" Clay asks.

"I'd love to say the romantic thing—that my heart led me back…"

Again, Grams blushes, and I swoon for her.

He chuckles. "Which is true…but I also know a few people in town."

Grams motions for everyone to follow her. "Let's all move to the dining room to eat."

Giancarlo and I hang back. His hands find my waist, and he draws me close. The scent of spice and soap hypnotizes me as I drape my arms over his shoulders. He presses a kiss to my neck, igniting a shiver down my back.

"You're something special, you know. Always have been."

I smile, but I also don't know what to say. I've never been great at receiving compliments.

"And you know what?"

"What?" I ask.

"You didn't just inspire Enzo, and your Grams. You inspired me. I'm convinced the only reason I got that mural done is because of you." He leans in and kisses my cheek.

The spot he just kissed warms then stretches through all of me. "You're the artist. I didn't do anything."

"Of course you did. If that's not enough proof for you, I did something else."

I knit my brows together, waiting for him to go on.

"I called my parents. It's going to be a work in progress, but I'm putting in the effort. I'm definitely going to Florida to visit my dad next year, and who knows, maybe Italy to visit my mom once we work through things."

I reach up and press my lips to his jaw. "I'm proud of you."

"What do you say to taking more chances together?" he asks.

"What do you have in mind?"

"My crystal ball sees an important day. A white dress. Maybe a home with a Shiba Inu, a travel companion, an ornament maker, and a muralist.

"I would take all of my chances on you."

He cups my face in his hands and leans in, his lips covering mine in a sweet kiss, my body buzzing.

Maybe this is a draft that isn't a standalone.

Maybe we're a series.

STAY IN TOUCH

I love hearing from my readers and seeing photos of them enjoying my books online! Tag me in your photos on
Instagram: (@racquelhenry)
Twitter: (@racquelhenry)
Facebook: (RacquelHenryAuthor)
TikTok: (@therealracquelhenry)

If you'd like to read a bonus scene with Felicity and Giancarlo, sign up for my newsletter! You'll also receive exclusive first looks, reading recommendations, access to subscriber-only giveaways, and all my writing news! Sign up here: racquelhenry.com/bonus.

ALSO BY RACQUEL HENRY

Juliet Washington left Orlando for LA five years ago to forget Ivan Underwood. When her company buys Ivan's magazine, she's forced back home to handle the transition—and what's worse, she must work closely with Ivan. Now more than ever she's determined not to let him get too close—he already broke her heart once.

After magazine editor, Ivan Underwood's boss informs him of a new parent company takeover, he never in a million years imagined the person handling the transition would be none other than Juliet Washington—the one that got away. At first, Ivan is looking for answers to the question that's been plaguing his mind forever:

Why did Juliet leave? But the more they interact, the more old feelings resurface, leaving Ivan even more puzzled. Does Juliet feel it too? For fans of Hallmark Christmas movies!

Note: This is a sweet romance novella, not a full-length novel.

Read *Holiday on Park*: racquelhenry.com/holiday-on-park/

After ten months of nursing a broken heart, Viola Evans is ready to move on—she just needs to let go once and for all. Determined not to let misery win, she resolves that she won't let anything get in the way of celebrating her favorite time of year: the holiday season. While participating in a Christmas activity one day with the children at her job, Viola writes a letter to Santa—surprising herself when she asks for someone new to make Christmas memories with. The question is, can she truly let go of the past and let love in again?

Charlie Palmer had to get out of New York City. After a confusing breakup with his ex, he makes a fresh start in Orlando. What he's not expecting to find is Viola Evans… or her letter to Santa detailing her deepest Christmas wishes. Drawn to Viola's charm and deep love for the holidays, Charlie finds himself wanting to give Viola the holiday memories she dreams of and Orlando starts feeling like home… that is until his ex resurfaces.

For Charlie and Viola, life has been complicated, but maybe all they need is a little holiday magic.

For fans of Hallmark Christmas movies!
Note: This is a novella, and not a full-length novel.
Read *Letter to Santa*: <u>racquelhenry.com/lettertosanta/</u>

Love. Christmas. Second chances. Heartbreak. Greyson Reeves. These are the things Chanel Baldwin has quit. As far as she's concerned, Greyson Reeves is The Grinch Who Stole Romance—a.k.a. the guy that broke her heart. Since then, music's been her main squeeze, and she's become one of the most renowned flutists in the world, traveling the globe for performances. When Chanel finally makes it home for the holidays, her meddling mother asks her to help write a song for the neighboring towns' annual "Song of the Season" Contest. All Chanel wants to do is get the holidays over with, but she agrees to help—only to discover that the person she's helping is The Grinch himself, Greyson. She's not expecting her heart to drop the equivalent of ten stories when she sees Greyson—or that the more time they spend together writing songs, the harder it is to stick to that quit list.

One look at Chanel after so many years and Greyson Reeves is done for, never mind how many times he's talked himself into believing their epic love story was over. It was his fault things ended anyway. Chanel was going to travel the world as a principal flute with cream-of-the-crop orchestras, and he was going to do the same as a conductor. It would already be tough to make it work, and he wasn't about to stand in her way back then. Fate had not ruled in their favor. And it broke his heart too. But now? Let's just say working with her for the annual Song of the Seasons Contest isn't just creating a song on paper but in his heart.

What if the same person who splintered your heart is the same one piecing it back together?

For fans of Hallmark Christmas movies!
Note: This is a novella, and not a full-length novel.
Read *Christmas in Cardwick*: racquelhenry.com/christmas-in-cardwick/

FOR WRITERS:

The Write Gym Workbook
The Writer's Atelier Little Book of Writing Affirmations

Racquel Henry is a Trinidadian writer, editor, and writing coach with an MFA from Fairleigh Dickinson University. She spent six years as an English Professor and currently owns the writing studio, Writer's Atelier, in Maitland, FL. In 2010, Racquel co-founded *Black Fox Literary Magazine* where she is Editor in Chief. Since 2013, Racquel has presented and moderated panels at writing conferences, residencies, and private writing groups across the US. She is the author of *Holiday on Park, Letter to Santa, Christmas in Cardwick*, and *The Writer's Atelier Little Book of Writing Affirmations*. Racquel's fiction, poetry, and nonfiction has appeared in *Lotus-Eater Magazine, Reaching Beyond the Saguaros: A Collaborative Prosimetric Travelogue* (Serving House Books, 2017), *We Can't Help it if We're From Florida* (Burrow Press, 2017), *Moko Caribbean Arts & Letters*, among others. When she's not writing, editing, or coaching writers, you can find her watching Hallmark Christmas movies.

Made in the USA
Columbia, SC
11 October 2025